Wendy Butler - Malta 2005

GW00703174

PEOPLE AND PLACES

ISBN: 99932-611-7-3

First published 2005
Text copyright © Michael Alexander 2005

JPS BOOKS
1 Alley N°1, Marina Street, Pietà MSD 08 - MALTA
Tel/Fax: (00356) 21 220 207, Mob: (00356) 7979 2324
Web: www.publishingcentre.com

For Gerda, Anna and Karel.

This novel contains actual facts which made it necessary to change some names of persons to protect their identity.

My thanks go to Barbara Upton for the translation of the poem by Sri Kabir.

The verses from Omar Khayyam are taken from J.B. Nicolas' translation "Les Quatrains de Khéyam", Paris, 1867.

CONTENTS

Here I am sitting on the balcony of my flat, sipping a glass of wine.

The evening sun shines with a reddish glow at the yellow-brown houses which seem to merge into one another. About one hundred meter distance, as the crow flies, the blue water of the yacht marina can be seen, palm trees and pines softly shake in a soft breeze. Shortly the yellow lights will be turned on at the sea promenade along the bay, followed by innumerable lamps in the houses. It is wonderful in Malta in the evening.

I think of N. who, out of the blue, came to see me in the afternoon. He always appears suddenly and unexpected. This time he left a small briefcase with me.

"I see you have luggage with you.We could go out for dinner. My wife is in Germany to see my son and my daughter-in-law. She will be back in a few days."

"No, thanks," he replied, "I have to catch a flight. But the contents of the case are for you."

"The contents?" I questioned carefully.

"They are diaries, old passports, documents, fotos, letters. You should go through them and do some writing," he explained with a smile.

"Not so fast. I am retired and don't write anymore."

"I know that," said N., "but this is something special. I want you to write my biography."

"I have never written a biography." I protested.

N. shrugged his shoulders," You can do this. And my regards to your wife.

"And," he added, "when you have gone through this," he pointed to the case, "you will think it over. But now I have to go, my taxi waits downstairs."

"And where are you going?"

"To India," he answered. "you will hear from me."

And with a friendly ciao he disappeared.

This is N. as I know him. We are of the same age and have known each other for almost half a lifetime. We studied together, although different subjects. I became a teacher and lecturer in history, working in Asia, Australia and Africa. He travelled as journalist through the same continents since 1952, when we both left Germany. We have been in constant touch and met each other in many countries.

I open the briefcase and discover forty-eight small diaries, neatly labelled and full of notes, twelve outdated passports, three boxes with photos, documents and letters.

How does one write a biography?

ON THE WAY OUT, January 1953

Telegraph poles whistle along. The lights of the train's compartment throw flashes of yellow on the soil behind the windows. A wide landscape, occasionally a few clumsy farmhouses with pregnant thatched roofs, skeletons of leafless trees look finger-black against the grey evening.

Brakes shriek in Bentheim: Customs on the German-Dutch border. German custom officials, very officious. (Wordplay: Is the traveller a customer?) They look into the passport, then look into a thick little black book to compare names. Luckily, N's name is not wanted.

The train slows down at the Dutch station. A big stamp appears in the virgin pages of N's passport: "IN".

A little Jew appears with a briefcase: "Currency exchange?"

N. exchanges a couple of hundred Deutschmarks. His profit is tremendous, but nu ja, nebbich.

The travellers crowd around the chocolate stall. Morning papers come along. The loudspeakers grumble something, and the train moves on.

On the left a Philips factory. Enormous glass windows. One can see the workers at their machines. Blue neonlights are jealous of the breaking morning.

The toilets smell of shaving lotion. Breakfast is served in the dining car.

"Well, you can catch the boat anyway, dear..."

"..habe ihm zu verstehen gegeben, dass die Umsatzkurve..."

"..to phone Roberts and Creel to send samples..."

"Café noir et cigarettes.."

3

"Dank u wel.."

"Zoits is uit de tijd, nietwaar?"

"..Humanity is faced with only two alternatives.."

"..quel eclat. Et mon père nàvait pas permis.."

"..is het nu eigenlijk, wat Spaak ons biedt?"

European Union at the breakfast tables.

The waiters juggle in between this salad of conversation with smiles, toast and silverpots.

The Netherlands are really one big town: Factories, vegetable gardens, tulips, backyards, main streets, stations, single houses, canals, pad docks, factories - that's the way it passes. One reaches Amsterdam without preparation.

N's preparation for all this was to get the contract with this Westgerman newspaper ("Kieler Nachrichten") to write human interest stories, features, opinions, to meet people...

First a hotel, than a stroll to find a travel agency.

He left his two suitcases in the room of the "Victoria" and went out.

Theatre Quarré, Rembrandts Plein, nice little restaurants. The sun shines somewhere. At Cook's the poster of the Pyramids look very attractive. "Centuries look down at you." (Napoleon)

How will it look today? Anyway, Egypt is his first assignment. "Passage to Port Said? Well, the Royal Dutch Mail leaves in six days, the Oldenbarnevelt, a nice ship. Of course you can pay in Deutschmarks."

Nice to have acceptable currency again, N. thinks, three cheers to Bonn. Bon.

"O.K., I take it. But I first have to get my visa."

A taxi brings him to the Consulate General. On the way he recalls the latest news. They just had a revolution there. The affair with King Farouk.

First thing he sees at the Consulate is a huge and pompous portrait of Farouk. Le roi est mort. Vive le roi.

"Visa? Certainly, but first I have to see the passage ticket."

Patiently N. explains that, on the other hand, the ticket is issued only after having obtained the visa. After some discussions the consul grins.

"Alright, tourist visa for three months."

It lasts one full hour, N. pays 20 guilders and goes back to Cook's. Second class cabin for 35 pound Sterling in exchange for Deutschmark.

The air in Amsterdam is mild for January. N. sits in the lobby of the Victoria Hotel. Hotel lobbies always excite him. One can sit for hours and play the old game: Guess who? He learned to play it in the subway. You simply look at people opposite you and guess their professions or jobs. In Hotel lobbies all adventure thrillers come to life: there are Bonvivants, Filmstars, Royalty incognito, con-men and foreign agents.

The young lady opposite flashes like lightning. N. resigns inwardly.

Too expensive. ("The worship of one leads to sorrow. But the love of the one in many is everlasting bliss").

The day before departure, N. takes in a Debussy concert at the famous Concertgebouw. "L' après midi d'un faun." Nymphs and salamander jubilee together with wind-spirits and those who live on clouds...

Afternoon of a faun in lazy sun glass and etheric dance of elfs straight from fairyland.

Beautiful. Just simply beautiful.

N. is lying on the lonely deck and looks the stars into their flickering eyes. The ocean below rolls a sea shanty. An atmosphere like in one of those tiny country-side chapels at Christmas time projected into a gigantic scale. It is like waiting for an angel coming from the maternal depth of the limitless space. Should one not say "In the beginning was space? Something without dimensions? Something which does exist out of itself?"

Each human being has ten power 14 cells. Each cell has a nucleus, which in turn consists of 48 chromosomes. Each chromosome consists of one-thousand genes, and each gene is composed out of one million of atoms.

And each atom has a nucleus, protons, neutrons and what not. How many atoms make one planet? And is, perhaps, the energy which makes the electric parts of the tip of one's little finger radiating, the same which makes the planets turn round the sun?

Ahoi, star-brother, we are of the same kind. N. thinks and remembers Lao Tse "Man is Universe on a small scale."

"Homesick?" a voice asks. Miss Doctor B. from Munich has the cabin next to his and a five year's contract with the Indonesian Government in her bag. She is enthusiastic to work in hospitals in the jungle. The ship's purser calls it the "Schweitzer complex."

"No, wanderlust," replies N. Nice kid, this young woman, frank and not sophisticated. The head steward placed them at the same table. All head stewards are pimps.

"Have you seen the dolphins?"

"Yes, when we passed Gibraltar something shiny played with the waves alongside. I first thought they were mermaid's."

Dr. B. smiles. "Dolphins are said to bring luck. You never told me what you are going to do in Egypt."

"Well," N. answered, "apart from my work, I am looking up some old friends, Echn-aton for instance, who gave notice to the priests because Egypt could get on without them. Or I'm going to prostrate in the desert dunes and worship the good old sun, caress softly the columns of the temple of Abydos, and bow before the Sphinx."

She looks at N. with a kind of medical radar.

"Don't you worry", N. laughs, "I am not a case. I love life and the world in my own way. Most of all I love space."

"- to forget?" she wants to know. Typical woman.

"Yes, - myself."

Again this professional look. "Please", N. continues, "why don't you go into the safety of a hospital at home? Why out into the jungle? You of all beings: young, nice, clean, with the best prospects for a great professional future. Why do you want to leave all that?"

"You are right," she says softly and leans back closing her eyes. C'est ca. Thanks God the moon is on vacation, otherwise it would have been a perfect situation a la Hollywood. N. smiles.

In the morning they played tennis on the sports deck. Two Asian military officers with babyfaces and sensitive politeness dissolved their match. They went to get some tea and had an argument about women's expenses. N. never understood why a woman will pay two pounds for a pair of stockings that are designed to make her look as though she isn't wearing stockings.

They laughed through to lunch with the peculiar happiness of children in a sandpit or elderly men in a bath tub. After lunch they played chess in the smoking parlour while the world was digesting. After dinner she went to see a movie, while N. was up on deck.

"Good night. See you in the morning."

And so he sits on a deck chair to welcome Africa.

He is alone with the noise of the ship's engine in her big belly, looking at the sea and the glow-worm-like reflections on the peak of the waves, alone under the endless nightblack sky, and the world belongs to him and he dissolves mind and soul in the magic presence of the stars.

The Great Architect of the Universe has created a desert. As if to soften His toughness He has sent a river through it. At one point, man has constructed a city. And here she is, with its new name: El Khahira, the victorious.

Narrow lanes, mosques with loudspeakers on top of their minarets, pompous houses, monstrous office buildings with cool marble lobbies, old citadels. Cars of all descriptions and vintages, camels, trams, donkey carts. The streets full of noise, hooting, flies and dust. With exception of wild motorcars everybody has time. And the heat forces you to have time and do everything leisurely. Yes, it is hot, the air is dry, the sky picturecard-blue and cruel.

Cairo fascinates everybody like Elvis Presley the teenagers. N. wonders how Cairo does it, and how long it will last. But Cairo works with the mystery of the East: From the Central station to the Birhat Bawaleh quarter, from the Sharia al Kubri to the Ibrahim Aga mosque - in Cairo prostitutes the Orient.

And, in the distance, the Sphinx looks at that, smiling and knowing that suckers are born one a minute.

Cairo once belonged to Egyptians, Greeks, Romans, Arabs, Turks, French, Englishmen - today it belongs to Thomas Cook & Sons and similar tourist agencies.

Standing on the roof of the Windsor Hotel in the Sharia Elfi Bey, N. looks down on the civilisation below. At the horizon a yellow-brown evil looking stripe: The desert.

" èssalaam aleikum -"

He thinks about all the Harun al Rashid stories (he, who sent a clock as a present to Charlemagne in Germany, although the Great

Charles was illiterate in 800 A.D.) and the Tales of the Arabian Nights. But books and films always forget the dust and the flies. Looking down into the canyon below he sees people running along like ants. Some don't seem to know where to go. Others carry parcels, pay cheques or themselves to their queen. Others go ashtray. But most of them, of course, are not ants but Orientals and, therefore, sit in a coffee house.

Do in Rome as the Romans do. Mr. Frey, the Swiss proprietor of this caravan oasis, smiles at N. on his way out.

Coffee houses are a masculine thing. Women cannot brew it properly in the Orient. And coffee in Arab countries has to be hot, sweet, strong, black and, anyway, there are never women in coffee houses to be seen except a very few female tourists at Groppi's.

"Khaffee masbouth -"

For Arabs the coffee house is the second home and place of business.

Here one makes the small and big deals. Here one receives friends and customers, partners and enemies. Here one is open for discussions, gossip and politics.

And here you meet interesting people.

And especially at Groppi's, one of the best known coffee houses in the world.

A middle aged European with glasses looked at N., smiling. He left his table and came nearer.

"You certainly must be German," he said in German.

"Yes." N. answered carefully.

"Mohammed Abdullah Abd el Mahdi." the stranger uttered.

"I do not understand," was' N. reply.

"Oh, that's my name. I just introduced myself."

"But you are European," N. stated.

The stranger smiled. "I was. I live here for the last thirty-five years and became Muslim. Therefore I have a Muslim name. Just call me Mohammed"

"Oh -" said N. and introduced himself.

"Every day I come here after work and have my coffee. And today I must meet you. But let us go to the Masonic Club at the Midan Opera to meet friends, you will like it there, wonderful people and good and cheap meals."

N. hesitated. Was this a new form of making contact for some dubious business? But then, Mohammed's eyes sparkled with that kind of genuine friendliness, that he agreed to come along.

On the way Mohammed talked about himself, happy to speak German again after such a long time. It appeared that he speaks fourteen languages including some native Arabic dialects. He had been professor at Prague University but had left Europe which he termed a crazy continent. And his work here?

"Well," he mentioned it almost casually, "I am Chief Supervisor at the Censorship Department at the Post office for all mail to Europe."

"So all my mails and reports go through your hands? I am a journalist."

N. showed him his Egyptian press card.

"Yes, that's right. If you want it dispatched quicker you just hand your outgoing mail to me." he grinned.

At Groppi's you can meet the most interesting people, N. thought. At the Masonic Club he was welcomed by a number of hospitable Egyptians after Mohammed introduced N. to them.

"And now, we go to my place. Its not far away, number 7 Kasr el Nil, almost round the corner," Mohammed insisted, "my wife will be delighted to meet you. But don't get frightened, she is very black, pure Sudanese and her great grandmother did know a good recipe how to cook humans. You know, humans are good if they are well prepared." he laughed. "But my wife is also a well known actress in the Egyptian film studios. Unfortunately she does not speak English or German. But we have a dog, three cats and the wall of one room is full of books, the other room full of clothing, obviously my wife's room."

N. was enthusiastic and agreed to go with Mohammed. People with many books and dogs and cats can´t be bad.

They move upwards in an old asthmatic lift to a sort of penthouse, containing two rooms, a pantry, a bathroom and plenty of terrace. On this they are welcomed by a dog and three wonderful cats, while out of the small kitchen a voice shouts "Mafeesh feelus, baba".

11

"This must be my wife, Hosna, she hasn't money left", Mohammed translates.

"Hosna?" remembers N., "I have seen her picture in a German magazine, where she was shown together with other Egyptian artists."

"Yes," Mohammed says, "it was the Stern-magazine, of April 1952, I think."

After introductions Hosna returns to the kitchen. The dog and the cats now demand attention and soon the hoarse voice of Hosna again: " - asah bhabab, Mohammed en erèbi alemani!"

They hurry into the bookfilled room, sit down on cushions on the floor and eat comfortably from a table designed for dwarfs a meal prepared for a king. Salaam - peace.

Hosna is a very agile woman with rolling eyes, whiten than white teeth, a motherly type. She knows to effectively wear European dresses, has a certain aristocratic flair and looking into her night black eyes one seems to imagine in them dark nights under acacia trees filled with mystical medicine-men witchcraft.

They have cool drinks made from pomegranates and play with the menagery: Tshubka is the friendly black dog of unknown ancestry, Bashibozu a grey longhaired tigercat with very selfconscious behaviour, Gummuriya is black with white and red stripes, named after the new Egyptian national flag. Her name means revolution, and, finally Mishmish, meaning apricot, and the colour of her hair is indeed ginger-pink.

Mohammed and N. discuss Europe and its customs.

"Do they still not have Time?" Mohammed asks.

"Yes" replies N.

"Miaou -" makes Bashibozu.

"Time is an invention of the human mind," lectures Mohammed, "believe me the Europeans will decline eventually with their obsession of time, the Americans anyway. One will save more and more time, quicker movements, faster machines - what for? And what will they do when they have caught up with time?"

"Maybe they will invent something else," N. remarks.

"- woof" Tshubka seems to agree.

Far away a red sun falls into the distant desert. The wind waves gently in tune with the callers for the evening prayer from the minarets. Dreamlike stars appear suddenly in the sky.

All these past weeks M. had been quite busy. Dr. Leheta from the press section of the Ministry for foreign affairs had been very helpful to issue N. with a press card. Nearly everyday was something new: Latest manifestoes of the Revolutionary Government, the dissolution of the Communist party declared by the military junta, army parades with tanks and units of the efficient desert police riding on camels, the Aswan project, the Suez Canal problem, the Sudanese question, finally successfully concluded by that ambitious officer, Major Saleh Salam, who yet behaved sometimes arrogantly towards the representatives of the foreign press.

Then an eye-opening conference with Pandit Nehru who came to Cairo on his way from London - and how he explained to the gasping Egyptians what international politics mean. N. made a mental note to interest himself a bit more for politics than his feature stories.

There was the special interview with old Amin El Hussaini, the exiled Grand Mufti of Palestine. From the fact that N. was kept waiting for nearly two hours being served with several cups of coffee as part of Arab ritual, he was not considered to be of great importance.

And then there were his new colleagues: Mr. Schusser from the German Press Agency (DPA), who asked N. to write him a feature on the status of women in Egypt, Ms. Ellen Brandt, a well known press photographer, Mr. Lacouture, a French journalist. N. was very pleased to be accepted by these "old hands".

One evening, he sat at the bar of Shepherd's Hotel with its age-old dusty velvet curtains and settled down with a sun-downcr, when a powerfully built man next to him addressed him in German: "You must be German, I think, at least you look it."

"Well, I am." replied N. "most probably because I have not achieved this particular suntan."

N. thought that it is not only part of his job but also because of his inclination to always make as much contacts as possible. "And," he added, "may I ask why you are here?"

"I am here for business," he smiled, "may be you have heard about me, I am Skorczeni."

N. was surprised. Skorczeni was the man who rescued Mussolini during the war, when the Duce was captured and held prisoner in a mountain hotel in Italy. It had been a daring coup using a glider to avoid the sound of engines.

N. enquired about Skorczeni's business and found that he now lived in Spain, owning a factory for small arms. Well, from a Nazi Heroe to a businessman selling small arms. This could be a story or better not.

Anyway, N's days were always filled with looking around, meeting people, watching out for small details.

And what is better than to have a look at the bazaar?

The famous Khalili Bazaar, for instance?

It stinks most unhygienic from dark corners, a hybrid collection of flies, guides, Greek merchants, Italian ice parlours, Sudanese shoeshine boys, Arab vendors, lunatic taxidrivers, effendis, beys, gullagulla-men, Panama-covered tourists from Venice, Illinois, USA, and more flies.

One can defend oneself after some time against beggars and vendors with sharply uttered words like "Ya ibn el khelb" or simply "Yallah".

But it does not work with the flies. Although living here for countless generations, flies don't speak Arabic. There is nothing left but to tolerate them stoically. One wrong movement on your part, and half a dozen vendors die to sell you fly whips.

Khalili Bazaar in Cairo. Here you can buy anything under the sun, almost like Harrods except for the elegance.

Dark bearded men whisper "foreign exchange?" Carpets, brocades, perfumes, hashish -, jetblack and soft brown eyes look at you, estimate, invite, advertise.

Dumpheap of civilisation.

"Scarabs, Sir?" a youth shows N. one of those green gems, carved in form of the mystic beetle which the ancient Egyptians put on the chest of their dead, "three thousand years old, guaranteed -".

"Yes, I know," N. answers in his first primary school Arabic,

14

"fabricated two blocks away by a modern machine made in Birmingham. Ana mafeesh tourist, Ali."

You can't cheat N.

Back at the hotel he finds that his passport has disappeared from his pocket. It is evening, he cannot reach the German Embassy. Without papers you are non-existent.

Mr. Frey tries to comfort him. "Did you have your address in the passport?"

"Yes, I put the hotel card inside."

"Then don't worry, the passport will be returned."

And at that precise moment a snug looking man, his eyes moving around, appears at the hotel reception, looks at N. and utters "Sir, I have found it. This must be yours." And he holds out a passport.

"Let me have a look," says N. and takes it, "yes, it's mine. Thank you."

"But, Sir, a bakshish -" N. looks at Mr. Frey who shakes his head. "Thank you very much again," repeats N. and puts his passport into his pocket. Mr. Frey gives the man a stern look, until he reluctantly leaves.

"Why couldn't I give him a tip?"

"Because this man was the thief. He cannot sell this passport anywhere, so he returns it to the hotel because our card was inside. He knew where to bring it."

Another lesson N. learned.

Next morning, with no appointments in his diary, N. remembers that he has been in Egypt for several weeks and hasn't seen the pyramids. Even Caesar and Napoleon - and besides they have three stars - the same as French cognac - in the tourist guide book. N. catches bus N° G from the Midan Tahrir to the Mena House Hotel in Gizah. Typically Egyptian that you don't tell the conductor the pyramids as destination for your trip but an oasis in which one has to drink tea if one claims to be one of the fashionable set. That's what the signboards advertise anyway which brighten up the majestic road to the pyramids in the truest and ugliest American fashion.

But the signboards are right as one is exhausted after the bus trip and simply is dying for some refreshment. N. goes into the Mena

15

House and really orders tea. Sitting on inviting rattan chairs on the terrace he looks at the many tourists, tired from dust, sipping unegyptian drinks and catching a glimpse of the yellow-red stone monsters between tropical foliage: the pyramids.

There they are, and the world sits at their feet and takes in refreshments.

Or writes picture postcards home with ecstatic exaggerations. Slowly, N. strolls through the desert and stops face to face with the sphinx who seems to grin from timeless height.

"Hiho, a human -"

What is your secret, creature composed from lion, eagle, bull and man?

N. thinks. Oh, your secret is the human secret, isn't it? Hidden in the royal chamber of our hearts. And we have to die a long inner death before we can enter. The entering into the royal chamber of the great secret of life and death is our initiation. An unseen voice whispers a word into our ear as the wind tells the desert sand the eternal story of creation. The wind carries it on as the messenger of the gods. Hermes, the wind. Hermes, the thrice-great, whispers the message into the ears of those who can listen.

All great philosophies of life have their origin in the contemplation of death. Life does not explain itself. But it fulfils itself after, not through, death. One has to die to know what life is.

Millions have faced you, Sphinx, fearful, ambitious, faithful, loving. You are old, Sphinx, older than science wants to admit.

For N. it is a tremendous experience: To sit on a clear morning amidst the yellow of the desert and meditate on the Sphinx. Shakespeare: "I am dyeing, Egypt. My spirit is going. I can no more..."

"I believe, you must be happy." a voice from heaven says.

"Happy?" N. answers slowly and looks at the Sphinx. "Perhaps. I think we really don't know when we are happy. Only when we ceased being happy we know that we were happy."

"You are a strange man," the heavenly voice remarks, "and I am hungry."

16

That can't come from heaven. N. turns round and instead of a fairy there is a young woman, blackhaired, which large fairytale eyes, olive tint and very fragile looking.

"Hi," N. recovers, "come to think of it, I am hungry too."

"Then let's eat."

N's brain immediately gives the air-raid warning: She wants to be invited, most probably into the expensive Mena House.

"My home is here on the Gizah road. Have lunch with me." she says simply.

"Accepted." N's brain gives the all-clear.

"My name is Heli."

"I am N." N. replies, "Heli - that sounds like Helios, like sun. And we are in the country of the sun."

"I am Copt," she states.

"Wonderful, so at last I am meeting a descendant of the true Egyptians."

She smiles and they walk through the desert sand towards Gizah which spreads itself out with lush gardens and well kept villas. They halt in front of Yasmin bushes and gravel garden paths.

"This is my little house," she points to a small house.

She is interior designer and painter. After the death of her parents she has bought this precious home.

"And why at the edge of the desert?"

"To be near my lover." she confesses.

"And who is he?"

"The Sphinx, friend of the cold North."

They eat, talk and talk and it seems that they knew each other for a long, long time.

Early mornings is the best time of the day to be near the pyramids. The sky is clear and the air is fresh. This is the time when thoughts emerge, one never quite knows wherefrom they come. During the day and working in dusty and noisy Cairo with its crowds of people there is no room for deeper and significant thoughts. On the other hand the evening with its glorious sunsets and the appearance of millions of stars - that is the time to relax, the time for contemplation of a different kind. The air is mellow, a small breeze promises coolness from the day's merciless heat. And once the full moon disappears, the stars will always remain.

It is the time for a sundowner or a glass of good dry wine.

"I like dry wine," remarks N., "although it is a silly adjective, because wine always is liquid."

Heli laughs and touches N's cheeks.

And so they develop a friendship which is rather unique. They both have a good sense of humour, of lightheartedness but also of thoughtfulness. For instance, if they talk about time-saving gadgets.

"The question is, what do we do in the time we save?" asks Heli.

"We remain wanderers to an unknown goal. And we have nothing against people who may call us fools," answers N., "there are two sorts of people who do not care to be called fools: These are the wise and the simple ones. What connects wisdom and simplicity? Our way of life has become full of diversity, we are complex, specialised."

"So let's be fools," Heli insists.

Of course, sex comes into their friendship too, but it does not play an important role. It is without demands, is soft and often only a minor episode in their form of comradery.

They both watch another sunset walking through the still warm desert sand. They hold hands so that they do not lose each other. One loses each other easier in the loneliness of the desert than in busy streets of cities. They hardly talk not to disturb the miracle. Worlds break up, centuries disappear like raindrops in the sand. Nothing remains but two people in the universe.

"Life is nothing but remembrance of times past, said Proust, but I can carry on his thought," N. remarks, "time past is nothing but confusion, a muddled impression,which leads nowhere."

"But, despite all this we have to make a living to secure our biological existence." retords Heli.

"Typical woman," N. laughs, "security comes first."

"No," says Heli, "first comes food. And for tonight I have something special which goes well with a glass of wine."

"Then let's go. I can hardly wait."

Back at Heli's house, N. busies himself opening the bottle while Heli prepares something in the small kitchen. She appears on the veranda with a large plate and toothpicks.

"This is a very old Egyptian snack," she explains, "way back from the old Egyptians. It was not called Egypt in those days but the land of Chem. These are Olives, marinated in oil and vinegar and covered with sesame seeds. The people at that time did not have toothpicks, but used their fingers. And with this snack they drank wine, although diluted with water."

"I think it tastes better without water," replies N. "but it is most delicious."

"Do you ever think of returning home?"

"My home is where I am," answers N., "going back? No. I feel that I have lost the fetters of past times. My inner clock does not show the historic time. The clock, at the moment is filled with Echnaton, dainty minarets, a wide sky, eternal pyramids, the mysterious sphinx, waving sand dunes and a wonderful woman."

"Thank you," Heli smiles, "but I feel you will have to go on into the future."

No, he would not go back. It would be cowardice. It is the uncertain future which makes life charming. Yesterday is a closed chapter, therefore not dangerous. Memory belongs to those who hesitate, who are afraid of tomorrow, of the new because they do not know what it will bring. And if they have to face the tomorrow, they do it with hopes, wishful thinking and prayers.

Tomorrow is the great unknown and, therefore, dangerous. But tomorrow is every second. The consciousness of danger sharpens senses and intuition.

The following day he told Heli that he had a contract with the Islamic Press Agency to travel to India which, of course, had wetted his appetite to discover new territories, new people and to enlarge his experience.

"In that case, I shall arrange a big farewell dinner to you and friends," Heli commented. And so she did.

Even in the Egyptian Gazette it was mentioned, that "she gave an enjoyable farewell dinner party on Saturday evening, September 19th, in honour to Mr. N., German journalist who will leave Egypt on October 1st for India. All the guests passed a very pleasant evening with an original Indian rice dinner.

Among those present were Dr. K.H.S., Mrs Ellen B., a well known magazine photographer, Mr. and Mrs. Lacouture, French journalists, and Mr. and Mrs. Schusser, the representative of the German News Agency DPA.

The day before N's departure they had a long evening together, walking along the lazy Nile. The large stars took a mirror-bath in the silent river. N. asked her not to come to the airport. He hated farewell scenes. They kissed good bye and emotions were put to rest.

It was N's first flight and he was quite excited. The Air India flight was scheduled to leave at 6.40 in the morning, so there was no time to sleep. He spent the night packing and took a taxi to be in time at the airport. And found himself among a huge crowd of people waiting to check in but never had heard of queuing. What fascinated him was the fact that not only the luggage, but also the passengers were weighted.

"Well, they have to know how much the plane can hold," someone said.

One rather well proportioned Indian lady was gently guided to the custom office.

"What's going on?" N. asked

"You must know that rather fat Indian ladies can hide anything underneath their saris. Usually there are gold bars carried in a belt around the waist." answered a seasoned fellow passenger.

After all the formalities were dealt with, flight no. All 116 left Cairo bound for Bombay.

Life seems to be a string of separations.

INDIA 1953

According to company rules, Air India's stewardesses embrace you when you land in Bombay. You are moved to bits, but in reality the company has retained this custom only so that the stewardess, while embracing, can feel your pockets with nimble fingers to find out whether you pocketed the silver cutlery as a souvenir.

N's first impression of Bombay airport? Sticky, moist, warm, the thick air filled with an exciting fragrance in which tropical flowers dominate.

N. was told that the south of the Indian subcontinent still conforms to the ideals (and prejudices) of Indian tradition, the tradition of Patanjali, Ramayana as well as of pre-Aryan origin. His mind, therefore, was all set on Madras, the metropolis of the South.

The passenger coach brings him and his suitcases through gushing and flooding monsunal cloud bursts to the railway station.

N. learned patience in Egypt. It is apart from a valid passport the most important thing in these parts of the world. He is, therefore, not at least annoyed that the next express train leaves for Madras in seven hours.

His funds allow him to purchase a first class ticket, sleeper. So he stays the hours in the restroom for first class ticket holders. These restrooms are equipped with comfortable settees, electric fans, shower rooms and conveniences. They are very quiet once the doors are closed. The noise outside beats the noise of Cairo. Indeed, Cairo is dead silent compared to an Indian railway station. He actually stays all the time in the restroom in the company of his suitcases because he feels a bit uneasy to find India different from what he expected it to be.

We humans, N. thinks, always prefer to hide from facing facts. That we cannot solve our problems because of that. And if there are some who truthfully call a spade a spade, convention jumps in and declares them inconvenient and not desirable.

With half an hour to go, N. takes his suitcases out to the platform and is at once surrounded by several bearers who all want to carry the luggage. N. chooses one of them, who snaps up the two cases, one on top of the other on his head and gestures N. to follow him. These bearers are clever and know exactly where to go to satisfy all the answers the poor white man may have. So he guides N. to a board where all the names of the passengers for the Madras express are listed according to the class. And to N's astonishment he finds his name printed on the lines for the sleeper 1st class. He points to it and the bearer goes on and stops suddenly on the platform.

"Train will be here and your carriage will be right here." he says in his sing-song English.

N. decides to stay put next to the bearer, surrounded by, it seems to him, crowds of people, tea carriers, sweet sellers and what have you.

Crowds with a mixture of hysteria, impatience, gaiety and resignation. People congregate waiting for the train or inspiration. There are areas of light, half-light, and shadows. Through these areas passengers sit on their luggage, walk or run around, bearers trot barefoot erect under headloads shouting warnings of approach. The platform floor is spattered with old and new spittings of betel-juice, which N. at first confused with blood stains.

But his astonishment grows even further when the train finally comes into the station and his sleeper carriage comes to a stand-still right in front of N. The door opens, a conductor appears, looking at N's ticket and guides him to his compartment, the bearer following with the suitcases, which he neatly stows underneath the lower bed. N. pays him, probably too much, but N. was glad to find himself in his new home for one night which he never could have found out himself.

He has a look around. A comfortable looking two-bed sleeper and, being the first to arrive, occupies the lower bed.

Everything looks clean, the air-conditioning is working, the lights are switched on, the table top can be lifted and below is a wash basin.

Quite satisfactory.

This is the second impression, N. has of India.

In Madras N. checks in at the Savoy Hotel, a small middle-class Indian Hotel at the corner of Mount Road and Whites Road. A very small room and a rather biggish bathroom, but clean and supplied with a huge ceiling fan which creates the illusion of a breeze.

Outside on Mount Road - the main road in this large city - he finds, not far away the Government of India office for Information, where a very polite clerk issues him the important press card.

"Well," he suggests, "you will not find much in Madras State about Muslim affairs, which the Islamic Press Agency demands from you.

You should go to Andra Pradesh State, to its capital Hyderabad. It is a Muslim stronghold. You should see the Charminar, a famous landmark, an imposing archway surmounted by four minarets, built in 1591.

And, of course, the great mosque modelled on the Great Mosque of Mecca.

And this state is ruled by the Nizam, you may want to interview him."

N. thanks him for the tip and strolls down the Mount Road, takes in the large advertisements in front of the cinemas with long queues of people, waiting at the box office to open. And at the end of Mount Road he comes across a wall enclosing an enormous site with one imposing entrance leading to an office block: Gemini Studios.

At the hotel he enquired about the Gemini Studios. The receptionist beams and tells N., that Gemini is the greatest film producer in the south, topped by only another one in Bombay.

N. thinks about features and decides why not do something about the film industry?

As a matter of fact, he did. And this was one of N's greatest success.

He met the proprietor (Gemini studios were privately owned), the eloquent, resolute business man, with artistic feeling, open hearted, not a snob inspite his millions: Mr. S. S. Vasan. He guided N. through the various studios of huge dimensions where films are produced simultaneously in different languages to be distributed to countries like Singapore, Kuala Lumpur, Ceylon, Bangladesh and, of course, all of the Indian subcontinent. "But," he explained to N., "in all our films there is no shooting and no kissing, because that would not be accepted by our code of behaviour."

And that gave N. the headline "SHOOTING AND KISSING FORBIDDEN".

This feature N. could sell to three Westgerman papers and one Swiss film-magazine together with photos supplied by the studios. In the following days Mr. Vasan invited him to a reception on the studio grounds, where N could meet the British writer Stephen Spender and others. And it was there that N. was asked whether he would accompany a camera crew to Kashmir. N., of course, accepted.

And a few days later he found himself crammed with dozens of people with their equipment divided into 3 small DC-3 planes heading north with a number of refuelling stops on the way.

Yes. there were breathtaking views - the famous Taj Mahal from the top, crossing rivers, bypassing Delhi, and, finally, reaching a military airstrip in Ladakh near the town of Leh. This was a sensitive area, forbidden to tourists, but, of course, Gemini Studios had a permit although valid for two days only. The crew frantically did their business, the air was wonderfully cool as it should in this altitude of over four-thousand meters. And surrounded by a splendid row of snow covered peaks reaching nearly seven-thousand meters.

Some Tibetans appeared from villages below on their small sturdy horses, put up nomad tents and preparing tea and food for the crew.

That was N's first meeting with smiling Tibetans. Their country, Tibet, lies behind this formidable mountain barrier.

After the days work, he sat with the crew tasting chang, the Tibetan homemade beer, which makes you quite dizzy after two or three mugs in this high altitude where the air is thinner.

There was not much time to go out in the ice-cold night and looking at the stars and start philosophical thoughts. Inside the tents, wrapped in thick blankets, one quickly went to sleep.

Early morning at sunrise the crew worked again on the shooting ready to board the planes in the afternoon, did some more shooting from the airplanes to get the mountain ranges from various angles - and off they went back to the south with its heat and humidity.

Back in Madras N. moved from the hotel to a small Indian style house in the suburb of Madras. Here, in Adyar, at Elliot Beach, he found it more convenient to write. It was calm and there was no disturbance from the chattering discussions of Indians at the hotel which, sometimes, went on during the night.

N. liked this small Indian thatched roof house facing the Bay of Bengal.

The room one enters from outside contained a wooden writing table, two stools, one easy chair, a bookshelf, a reading lamp and a table fan. The window had iron bars and wooden shutters to keep unwanted visitors away. The second, adjacent room, had a wardrobe, a bed with a mosquito net positioned over four corners of the bed, a bedside table with a reading lamp, a chest of drawers was the place for an electric cooker.

From there a door led to a high-walled courtyard with a water tap on one side which served as a shower. All floors were of concrete and all walls were whitewashed.

This little simple house was surrounded by high and slender palmtrees and between the house and the beach casuarina trees gave some shade.

N. soon found out that the best time was very early in the morning when a red sun was rising out of the ocean and cool wind was blowing gently, giving way, after a few hours, to the moist heat of the day.

The other pleasant time was after sunset when a refreshing breeze made the humidity agreeable.

It was simple but beautiful. He could write in this calm surrounding and, above all, he found time to think. To think and "perchance to dream".

The past weeks he had been getting around. In Hyderabad he interviewed the Nizam, and the five carat diamonds on his earlobes strangely fascinated him. He had gone to Pondicherry, formerly a French possession with its quaint French architecture, to Masulipatam, to Madurai with its carved temples and where a Hindu pandit taught him the Gayatri, the universal prayer to the sun, (which he found an astonishing parallel to Pharaoh Eknaton's ode to Aton, the sun.) he went up to Delhi with its chaotic traffic and bustling crowds of people.

He met "very important" and less important people from all walks of life...

In short: India bewitched him. He was in love with India, found it intoxicating. India, with all her spontaneity and primitive dynamic is also full of innocence. An innocence long forgotten in the West. The white sahib should really learn that it is not always reason that leads to the best in all he does.

To listen to the melody of this great, mysterious, extraordinary country and its manifold people is capable to open up new vistas. Meeting India, without comparing, sets free forces which made N. grow far beyond the convictions and conventions which so far ruled his life.

And here he now sits in his little house listening to the waves of the Bay of Bengal digesting all these impressions, dreaming and here he wrote his first poem:

> Let me taste the silence
> that flows behind your dark eyes.
> The bird is heavy on the hill,
> and the silence
> fills its black vessels of sound.
> The golden ladder of love
> leads to your rooms.
> And my hands are flowers,

falling with the beat of the sea.
The world is vast -
and you are watching through the split in
the leaves.
Down, my soul,
into the night without desire,
where the reflections are no more,
where all rooms are broken into the vast
space.

DIVERTISSEMENT

It was middle December 1953 when I arrived in Madras. I had received a scholarship to research and write my thesis on "The Protection of British-India by economic, political and military Means" and another paper I wanted to do was a translation into German from an ancient pre-Buddhist script and to write a commentary.

I was allowed to use the magnificent Library of the Theosophical Society in Adyar and to rent a room there at Olcott House within a short walking distance from N's little house. As a matter of fact it was I who mentioned this house and persuaded N. to move from the noisy hotel in Madras.

So we met quite often and had wonderful times. Christmas eve we sat on the beach and celebrated with a bottle of whisky which I had brought from Germany.

"The last drink I had was in Cairo, ages ago," remarked N. "but the prohibition in India will soon be abolished, I have heard."

"And what is your impression of India" I wanted to know.

"It's great. I still have not discovered all I want. My difficulty is with the English spoken here."

"You mean the peculiar raising and lowering of pronunciation?"

"No, I got used to that. I mean the words they use, almost Victorian. You know what a stepney is?"

"No."

"A stepney is a spare wheel or tyre. You know what a dickey is?"

"Well, I only know that it is slang and Queen Victoria would not have been amused if she had heard it."

"You are quite wrong. I dickey is a rear-facing spare seat in a carriage, applied today for a car's boot. This is not English, it is

29

Hinglish. These old words are a left-over from the British Raj. It consists of words never discarded. They go on forever, sometimes cherished and often abused but never thrown away. Instead they are mixed with mildewed British soldier's slang and that makes up Hinglish." so N. went on.

"I give you an example: You do not leave town here, you go out of station.

You put up rather than stay at a hotel. Nothing in India happens three times, it happens thrice. A politician would not dream of simply withdrawing a statement but would, on reflection, decide that it was infectious and resile from it. Hire-purchase is called here hypothecation. And you pay a quantum of rupees not an amount."

So we laughed in these late evenings fanned by a mild breeze and enjoyed it.

On other times the conversations were more profound.

"I had read in the paper that Krishnamurti has left Madras. Did you interview him?"

"I met him," answered N., "but I did not interview him. I attended six of his lectures, always very early mornings. We sat on the ground on mats and the place was always full. And, very un-Indian, the crowd sat silently. One day, though, there appeared police and some sharp looking civilian dressed Indians and searched for someone in the crowd. And they found him. It was Nehru, the Prime Minister. He had slipped out of Government Guesthouse where he had stayed overnight. And his body-guards had been either asleep or absent. Someone had found out that he always had been impressed by Krishnamurti. We heard this story after this."

"How did you find Krishnamurti?" I asked.

"Difficult to put into words," N. replied, "You see, he smashes your brain to bits until you have the feeling your brain has given up, has gone. And all this in a mild voice. The interesting thing is you don't need your brain to understand him. You do it with intuition. Yes, I wanted to interview him and got an audience. Krishnaji sat on a stool and drank a glass of orange juice. He pointed to another stool, I sat down.

'Well?' he asked. 'I have no question to ask,' was all I could say. We just looked at each other. His smile was radiant, his eyes very gentle.

'You should see my school in the Nilgiri Hills,' he suddenly spoke. I got up from my stool, bowed, thanked him and went.

I have never met a person like Krishnaji, a person who completely rested within himself. He is a great man, and no wonder that he inspired people like Aldous Huxley - you should read his novel "Island" - and Professor Erich Fromm, a famous psychoanalyst."

"Now, tell me," I asked on another occasion, "we have both gone to India for different reasons, but what are you going to do?"

"I shall stay here till the end of this year and than I shall move on, most probably to Pakistan."

"And after that?"

"Another country, meeting people and places. How do I know now?"

"You are quite adventurous."

"It is in my family," and here N. smiled, "may be I am genetically conditioned.

One uncle of mine volunteered to service in China to help to correct the Boxer mutinee for European powers, that was, I think in 1909. But he did no active part, he fell in love with a Chinese girl, married her and my family never heard from him again. Another uncle travelled for reasons never known to us, to South America, shortly before the first World War. We did get a postcard from Manao. He disappeared. The next was a cousin of mine I knew quite well. He was interested in mysticism and his wish was to join dancing derwishes somewhere in the Caucasus region. He managed to get transferred to a unit during the Second World War and he actually reached southern Russia, and from there he deserted and was never again heard of. He may have found his derwishes.

I just tell you that there is a certain tendency in our family for playing with adventure, for not accepting traditional conventions, the sudden stepping out of bourgeois security into a life which consists of many question marks.

One of my relatives, though, did return. Probably, because his adventure was not voluntary. This uncle of mine was taken prisoner in Russia during the first World War, spent eight years in Siberia, was freed by Czech troops and reached Germany via Japan. He reported most interestingly of wide steppes between Tomsk and Irkutsk, dream-nights at Lake Baikal.

He survived the time as prisoner of war by teaching the Russian guards football. The guards were almost also prisoners in their job, they were bored and glad to get distracted. So my uncle, who was a sports teacher, coached them and played the part of referee for seven long years.

These stories filled me with wanderlust. My most loved book of childhood up to adolescence was a world atlas, later I got a globe which was even more fascinating. I became a dreamer of many adventures in all corners of the world.

That should answer your question."

Indeed it did.

INDIA 1954

N. stirs from a deep sleep. Something must have been fallen on the roof. There is a scratching noise. Something has fallen through the roof, and has landed right in the middle of the mosquito-net which, through the impact, curves down on him. Something now nests heavily on his belly.

N. carefully pulls back his side of the net and switches on the bedside lamp. Now he is fully awake. The something is a fairly long green snake curled up contentedly on N's warm body.

Very slowly he manages to crawl out of bed, trying not to disturb the snake. He gets hold of the four corners of the net, knots the ends together and looks at his catch. The snake looks at him, the thin tongue playing nervously.

We both had a shock, thinks N., you don't look like a nasty beast, but nevertheless -. He carries his catch into his backyard and closes the door.

He manages to go to sleep without the mosquito net.

Next morning his houseboy wakes him preparing morning tea. (Strangely the servants were always called "boy", although he is well over fifty.)

"There is a snake in the yard, Babu. I caught it in my mosquito net. It came through the roof."

Babu looks at the ceiling and then goes out to the yard. Coming back he grins "I take a look-see. It is very harmless tree snake.

Must have fallen from long palm tree, may be was drunk. I call someone from village to mend roof. No worry, Sahib."

Babu then goes back into the yard, takes the net, carries it through the bedroom and the front room and disappears. He returns after a while with the empty net.

"I found nice place in the grass for snake to sleep off. I do not kill animals." And with these words he starts to position the net back onto the four poles.

Another new experience of India, N. thinks.

He had heard about snakes from the village elder. In the small village within easy walking distance from his house there grows a Banyan tree with a hole between its roots. Every morning the village headman carries a bowl of milk and places it next to the opening. When N. had asked him, he replied: "There is a cobra living there. Cobras are the kings of the snakes and very holy. They are useful to us, they catch mice so our grain storage is safe. That is why we bring it milk"

There had been another encounter as well. All his washing N. gave to the village dobhi who collected them once a week. But his shirts he washed himself, when he gave them to the dobhi he would return them with all buttons missing. As in that climate one has to change shirts at least three times a day, he usually put them on a line in his courtyard. One morning there was only one shirt left. Looking around and up to the tall palm trees he saw happy monkeys playing around with his now torn shirts. From then on he hung them out during the day when the monkeys had their siesta.

So much for N's experience with Indian wild life.

And then N. discovered that near his place was the site of one of the most famous dance academies, the Khalakshetra, run by a renowned principal of classical Indian dance, Srimati Rukmini Devi.

It was quite an enterprise. The young eleves were between 13 and 18 years old, there was a boarding school, a dance studio, a small weaving factory where most beautiful gold brocaded saris were produced.

N. could attend some dancing lessons and rehearsals and admired the classical Bharatya Natyam where nimble fingers would show a variety of gestures, movements, Mudras each symbolically interpreting feelings, signs, heavenly symbolic stories with stamping feet on which small bells accentuated rhythm - it was simply beautiful and N. could sense the devotion to Shiva, the dancing god of the Indian world of gods.

Dream-time again. But watching the slender girls N. remembered that kissing and shooting are "verboten!"

The dreaming part comes to a sudden halt when, on the way to the bus stop, a lorry did not brake in time, N. falls down on the dusty road bruising his arm and his head.

He has difficulties getting up, his vision gets flurry. Some people help him up.

"Doctor lives here", one man shouts and they carry him to the doctor's house. N. sees all this through a fog.

"Accident", he mumbles feebly. The doctor seems to agree, examines N's head and arm. Another, a nurse? cleans his bruises from blood and dust.

"I shall give you a tetanus injection."

He makes N. lying down, the nurse holds his head and the doctor does his job while N's consciousness slowly disappears.

But, a short while later, he slowly opens his eyes, he sees a heavenly face smiling at him, holding his head to make him sit up.

"I am Lakshmi, doctor Subramaniam's daughter."

"Thank you very much, you are very - (beautiful, he wants to say) - kind."

The doctor returns and also smiles.

"You should be alright now. Stay for a cup of tea."

N. introduces himself, they talk, some houseboy brings tea on a tablet while Lakshmi pours it into cups.

And so begins a friendship. Dr. Subramaniam has studied in Edinborough when India still belonged to Great Britain and still works as a practitioner here in Adyar. He is a soft spoken man, highly intelligent and prefers the simple life, is an admirer of Krishnamurti, and so N. has much to contribute as well.

"What do I owe you?"

The doctor waives it aside.

"Nothing, to make your acquaintance is quite enough."

On the way out Lakshmi accompanies N. to the front door.

"You know, I have never held a head of a European," she says shyly.

"But you did it quite nicely. Is it possible to see you again?"

"Perhaps."

"You know where I live?"

"Yes, you told my father."

So they part - N. still feels a bit weak and decides not to go to Madras but rather goes home for a rest.

In the afternoon someone knocks at his door and N., for a moment, thinks of Lakshmi, but this was wishful thinking or? Outside stood Dr. Subramaniam's houseboy with a piece of paper.

"Chit from doctorji," he says. "and I have reply, yes?"

N. nods and reads what the note says.

"Dear N., will you join us tonight at the concert given by Ravi Shankar which starts at 6 p.m. under the great Banyam tree at the compound of the Theosophical Society.?"

"Tell doctorji I will be there at six o'clock."

The houseboy salaams and trots off.

The great Banyam tree. N. knows the place. It happens to be one of the largest and oldest in India. The fairly thick air roots look like Gothic columns and give room for over a hundred people.

The Adyar compound consists of a number of large well built houses, a wonderful large park with interspersed temples, mosques, churches of all religions peacefully together, a small lake with lotus flowers and an overall atmosphere of tranquillity and peace.

In the evening N. sits crosslegged, like all the other many people on mats under this natural roof of the magnificent Banyam tree. To his left is Lakshmi, dressed in an ankle-long frock. She wears a choli and her arms and part of her midriff are bare. The little red tika between her eyebrows beautifully accents the shape of her oval face. Her father sits to his right looking forward to the small emporium where now the tabla player arrives, putting his two drums before him. Right behind comes Ravi Shankar carrying his sitar.

The sitar is a traditional Indian lute having seven main strings and further twelve sympathetic strings, it is about over one meter long, originating thousands of years ago from Persia.

They both squat on the podium and fold their hands to the Indian greeting. The audience is calm, there is no applause, because that would utterly spoil the beauty of this place.

And in this silence, full of expectation, he takes the instrument and softly plucks the first strings. The twelve sympathetic strings vibrate freely. It sounds like bird's calls in the very early morning, when they awake and greet the new day.

These first melodies open up one's heart. Then the tablas start with a soft rhythm. Then the sitar again, becoming more fiery, tablas and sitar together have a furious dialog, ending sweetly in beautiful harmony.

"Everytime I listen to Ravi, I never hear the same music. Everytime it is improvised," whispers the doctor, "just like a jam session."

The audience is spellbound as the concert goes on and at the end of one hour one gets up and slowly moves home. No words are exchanged, everybody almost experienced a spiritual happening.

"Yes, this music is a spiritual, a religious worship."

Next day, in the evening, Lakshmi appears at N's door, but not alone. Her sister is with her.

"I can't come alone," she says, "it is not our custom."

N. understands. "But your sister is also a nice chaperone." They sit together, drink tea, talk - but no more.

Another Indian experience for N. And then, they depart. A colourful butterfly, just passing by...

"True hearts have eyes and ears, no tongues to speak. They hear and see and sigh, and then they break." (Sir Edward Dyer). " Well, Lakshmi -" says N. to himself, "tu est un papillon brun. Moi, je suis blanc. Mais nous sommes les prisonniers de la bonne fortune." (J. Avéry)

On his last days, N. meets a couple belonging to one of the twenty-three families who practically own Pakistan: The Minwallas. They are not just one Parsi family, they are a whole clan of landowners, industrialists, hoteliers and what have you. These two Minwallas attended a conference in Adyar and were delighted to hear that N. would come to Pakistan on his next assignment.

37

"You must come and see us. Where will you stay?"

"In Karachi, but I don't know yet where."

"You stay at the Metropole Hotel. My uncle owns it," Mr. Minwalla orders, "I shall tell him and you will get special rates."

Four days later, N. sits in the lounge of Bombay Airport. Three hours of waiting, next to an elderly Englishman of military bearing with a typical moustache of a retired British officer.

"You live in Bombay?" N. asks.

"Yes, indeed I do. Waiting for a friend to arrive. I lived many years in India. When I was in Poona - stationed there - those were the days."

"I imagine, they were," N. remarks, "life is always better in a colony."

"Well, listen, I came out in 1935. In those times I was young, I believed the world belongs to me. I was privileged, because I was taught at the public school to think we should rule by divine right."

"And why do you stay on in India?"

"I retired in 1946 with rank of Colonel. I am a widower. Why should I go home? I can live nicely on my pension out here. I get my morning tea, I get my tiffin regularly, and in the evening I go to the expratiate's club, not to be compared with our real clubs in the old days."

"But, you see," he adds, "India has some magic. It catches your soul."

"I understand you quite well," says N. "I have been here only two years, but I got the bug too. And, surely, I shall come back."

His departure is announced by a creaking loudspeaker.

"Nice to have met you. I am off now."

"Bye."

Yes, N. thinks when boarding the plane, I certainly will come back some day.

But now for Pakistan, a new country, new faces, what is waiting for him?

And suddenly, by sheer intuition, N. feels that the real adventure is waiting ahead.

PAKISTAN 1954

With squealing tyres the black car turned around the corner from the Palace Hotel towards the bridge leading to the Beach Luxury Hotel. It was one of these sticky, humid nights in Karachi, the streets nearly empty. N. walked the few meters to the car which had stopped with dipped headlights. The large thick envelope stuck on his skin under his shirt. It not only was the humidity but the anxious expectation which caused him sweating.
As soon as he jumped in, the car quickly drove on.
Kuimov sitting next to N. in the back turned around several times and then made himself comfortable.
"No reason to be excited," he said smiling, took out an etui and offered N. a cigarette.
N. took it, thanked him. He was afraid that Kuimov may have seen the sweat drops on his face when he lighted his cigarette.
"Where do we go?" N. asked.
"On a roundabout way to the embassy," Kuimov answered, "you did bring the material?"
N. felt the wet envelope under his shirt and nodded. These are the moments in life which one experiences intensely, which one always will remember, N. thought, this is one of those moments. The car - an old Opel or a Zim? - drove very fast through empty streets, so fast that N. did not recognize which direction the driver was taking. Occasionally Kuimov looked back but nobody was trailing them. He spoke a few words with the bull-necked driver and leaned back. N's heartbeat had calmed down.
Now he could recognize some of the streets. They had reached Clifton and turned into Bleak House Road. A very rich part of

Karachi, embassies, manor-type villas surrounded by high walls, many street lamp-posts.

"Put your head down," Kuimov whispered suddenly. N. bent down so that his head was almost on his knees. There was a gleaming flare of floodlights, then darkness.

"You are alright now," Kuimov said, "we are there."

The floodlights were shining on the entrance of the wall, obviously put on by the Pakistani so that they could observe who enters the embassy.

The car moved on to the back of the building and stopped in front of a door. Kuimov left the car, walked around and opened the door on N's side.

"Please," he said like a well groomed chauffeur.

Some unseen person must have opened the door of the building. They walked in through corridors. Kuimov opened one of the oldfashioned doors.

"So, here we have it cosy," he remarked and pointed to a number of settees with sidetables full with bottles:Juices, soda, Coca-Cola, whisky, vodka, wine, liquors, cigarettes of all kind of brands, ashtrays.

"Please, make yourself comfortable." N. saw that none of the bottles were opened. Was that a hint that they were not manipulated?

Kuimov looked at N. and smiled.

"You do not have to be afraid, nothing is manipulated. Help yourself."

N. took one of the cigarettes and inhaled deeply. He opened the top buttons of his shirt, took out the wet envelope and handed it to the Russian.

"This is the material, at least the first part," N. explained, "more will come if you want it."

Kuimov took the envelope and said: "You will understand that we have to check the content first."

"Of course," N. replied, "but you will find that it is valuable. I do not cheat you."

"We don't want that either," Kuimov smiled, "you will get the value paid in cash, when the content is of interest. How much -"

"This material is worth 5000 Rupies."

"That much?" Kuimov's eyebrows started going up.

"I need 5000 if you want more," N. answered.

"We shall see." Kuimov moved towards the door, "just a moment and please, help yourself."

N. noticed that he did not hear the sound of a click. So the door was not locked. But, who knows whether there are cameras hidden away. N. remained seated, helped himself to a cigarette. It did not take long when Kuimov returned and sat down.

"I have to return the material tonight, as arranged," remarked N.

"Certainly," said Kuimov, "we are interested that everything works without difficulties. It will be photocopied and analysed now. Would you like a drink?"

"Just some water, please."

Kuimov opened one bottle of Schweppes and filled two glasses.

"Of course, we have to know more about you, especially how you come across this material, with whom you work together, and why you contacted us. It is important that we know each other."

"Well," replied N. and smiled, "I also would like to know with whom I work. The KGB?"

"Sorry, I must disappoint you. We are the GRU, the Soviet Military Intelligence."

N. took his passport out of his pocket.

"Here is my pass. I am not the distributor of this material. I am the deliverer only, sort of a postman. You know from the material from where it comes: The Americans are building these airstrips. The building is done by privately owned construction companies. The man who leads the construction team of the runways is not an American but a German. We are friends and we need the money. We thought who might be interested and would be able to pay. So we decided on you. I, therefore, went to your embassy -"

"I know," Kuimov interrupted, "that was very risky. Now, what is the name of your friend?"

N. shook his head. "You only have to deal with me. In any case I would have to consult my friend first. He also does not know your name. I only told him that I am in contact with an official of your embassy."

"Well, we shall talk this over another time," Kuimov replied.
At that moment there was a knock at the door. Kuimov went to the door, opened it just to take two envelopes and closed the door. "I understand that you gave us only every second page of these construction descriptions and one blueprint."
"That is correct," answered N. "the other pages you will receive next time."
"You don't have to be suspicious," remarked Kuimov, "we are quite civilised. So here are your passport and the material and in this envelope is the money you had asked for."
N. thought quickly, whether he should count it but decided against it. He put both envelopes inside his shirt.
"We shall take you back wherever you want," offered the Russian.
"Somewhere at Elphinstone Street. We could meet day after tomorrow, but please not at the same place as today,. Could it be at midnight on the parking area in front of the Palace Cinema?"
Kuimov thought for a moment, then he nodded.
"O.K., I agree. Now we have to go."
They left the embassy. The car waited for them at the side door. N. again bent his head down when reaching the front portal with the lights without being told so. Quickly they passed the Clifton bridge and headed via Victoria Road into Elphinstone Street. Just behind the Chinese restaurant N. asked to get out. Kuimov let the car stop, N. got out and the car went off at a very fast speed. N. entered a small lane which led towards the bazaar, stepped carefully over sleeping beggars and reached the boarding house where Kreisel was living.
The dirty glassdoor was open, as usual. A dim bulb gave some light to the entrance hall. The chaukidar slept on a mat and snored. N. softly went on to the first floor and knocked at Kreisel's door. He heard some papers being moved, then Kreisel opened the door.
"Well?" he asked.
N. smiled and put the envelope with the money on the bed, sat down on the only fragile chair and opened his shirt wet from perspiration. He also took out the other envelope with the papers, lit a cigarette and reported.
Kreisel was enthusiastic.

"And day after tomorrow the second part?" he asked satisfied. N. nodded. There were blueprints, charts, details of airfield constructions, runways and underground installations all over a small table.

"You are still working at this time?" N. enquired. He could never get used to this hole of a room, could not understand how Kreisel, a man of some position in his field, could live in this drab place.

"It is the only quiet time," Kreisel replied.

N. yawned and got up.

"I go to bed now. We meet day after tomorrow in the afternoon at the Metropol. All right with you?"

Kreisel agreed, counted half of the money and gave it to N. N. put the money away and disappeared quietly and and fast as he had come.

Back on the street he had to climb again over sleeping people on the pavement, went through the small Peoples' Park with its limp, listless and dusty palm trees, and reached his boarding house which is proudly called Sartaj Hotel.

Two days later, the people are just leaving the cinema at Club Road, when N. mingles with the crowd. The street traders are selling sweets and samosas from their small carts. Somehow N. feels more secure here but has difficulties to spot Kuimov's car among the taxis, private cars and motor rickshaws which take up the narrow parking space.

But finally he finds it and jumps in. The car cannot move quickly.

"Good evening," Kuimov greets him, "this place is not good for our purpose." He feels at ease once the car finds its way .

"You are right," N. remarks. They now drive on the extension of Elphinstone Street.

"Do you see the trees on your left side? There, the third tree next to the letter box. We shall meet here in exactly one hour from now. Have you got the material?"

N. opens his small briefcase which he had taken this time and handed over the papers. They compare their watches, he gets out and the car speeds ahead.

N. stands alone on the street and is not sure what he could do. Slowly he returns to Club Road. Some people still stand at the street traders´carts and eat. Some beggars come near him, so he quickly walks towards the Metropol Hotel. The hall is nearly empty, only a few Americans have a dispute with the night porter. The dining room was closed, in the bar some guests have drinks, N. looks around but does not know any of them.

The cane settees in the inner yard are empty, and N. walks back to the road. Next to the Hotel was the German Reading Room. Here Kreisel had given him the papers in the afternoon.

N. walks on to the corner of Victoria Street. There is no light from the windows of the first floor flat of Doctor Z. It was there where N is a usual visitor to the family, playing chess, having a meal and afterwards playing mah jong with the family.

The small coffee shop next door is closed too. The night is warm and sultry. Very few people are to be seen. N. looks at his watch: Just twenty minutes had passed. So he walks on, down Victoria Road, turns right into Elphinstone Street where some show windows have their lights on. And then back to the meeting point. Few minutes before the arranged time he stops at the third tree next to the letter box. Suddenly he hears a motor. He turns around, the driver switches the lights off and comes slowly nearer. Kuimov opens the door, N jumps in and the car speeds on.

Kuimov returns the papers and an envelope. "Here is the material and your money," he explains, "and please sign this receipt."

He gives N. a piece of paper.

"I can't read it, it is Russian. How can I sign it?"

"Well, we have bureaucracy too. I need the receipts for the amount we have paid you so far. You can sign with your code-name, if you want."

"My code-name?"

"Yes," Kuimov smiles, "I have baptised you Mohammed."

N. laughs and signs.

"When do you have the next pages?"

"I can't tell you now. My friend will have a chance to get at the material in a few days time. How can I reach you?"

Kuimov explains the procedure. "You know our telefon number. If you have the material you call exactly at twelve noon the embassy. You let it ring three times and hang up. This you repeat two times. I shall be at the phone every noon. When it has rung nine times I know it must have been you and that you have the material. We then shall meet at eight in the evening at the same spot as now. Agreed?"

"Yes, of course. But in future we should like to have the amount of money in foreign currency, dollar or pound sterling."

"It is all right with me." Kuimov says.

This time Kuimov lets him out at Bunder Road, and N. quickly walks to Kreisel's boarding house.

He seems to have waited for N. He sits on the bed and waives N. to the chair.

"Successful?" he asks.

"Business as usual."

"Except that we get the money in foreign currency and not in Rupees."

"Very good," smiles Kreisel. N. takes out the papers and the money from his briefcase which they divide. N. looks at the table and notices the blue prints from last time.

"You did not have to return them?" N. wants to know.

"I have got them copied with permission from the top."

He unfolds the big plan and explains: "This is the overall plan of one airfield. The smaller plan is of the runway only. The exact calculations of the strength of concrete are clarified in the material which I gave you today. These are very important because from that our friends can see for which aircraft the runways are conceived. But this is only one airfield. We are going to build four or five others as well. Which means that we are in business for some time."

"I have to go now, let me know when there is more to come. I am always in the German Reading Room in the afternoon."

Slowly N. goes down the stairs. Everything is quiet except for the snoring of the chaukidar in the dimly lit hall.

The bazaar workers, the bearers and the beggars sleep on their mats.

Thoughtfully N. goes into his boarding house.
Despite a cold shower he still feels not refreshed. He goes to bed but cannot sleep. He has an idea which slowly grows on him. How did all this develop?
When N. landed in Karachi airport he at once smelled the difference. In India it was the smell of cows and the fragrance of flowers and spices.
In Pakistan it was the smell of camel urine and spices. While the cows were only hindering the flow of traffic in India, the camels in Karachi had to pull slowly heavily packed carts while chewing, grunting and sometimes spitting.
Later on there were funny episodes with these camels. The Americans, while fullfilling their military aid to Pakistan which included a mass importation of trucks, more or less ordered the government to introduce right-hand-traffic. So for weeks the population was trained, taxi drivers and other users of streets were prepared by media, new street-signs were put up, traffic police gave advice that one has to drive on the right side of the roads, that one had to overtake on the left and that, finally, even traffic lights were to be installed. Lastly, the big day had arrived.
The whole police force was on alert. With much arguments and loud voices the whole new order worked surprisingly well - apart from the camels. They had been trained for ages to keep to the left and they stuck to it stubbornly as camels are. There was no way to lead them to the right side. They arrogantly looked at the humans and remained on the left. Whereupon the town council of Karachi gave in, cancelled the right-hand traffic and everything remained as it was.
The camels were victorious.
The media were delighted, the foreign press chuckled. That's Karachi.
Karachi, at that time the capital city of Pakistan, was in many ways a funny city - at least in the eyes of N.
Like in India even the smallest shops used high-ranking names. There was a factory producing fountain pens calling itself "Golden Industries", a small grocery shop was named "The New World Emporium".

But the best one N. found in Elphinstone Street: A tailor who sold material and custom-made suits to men and women had a sign reading: "Ladies get fits upstairs."

Soon after his arrival he paid a courtesy call to the German Embassy. As a journalist it was always wise to do so. They were very enthusiastic in having a new arrival, because the German expatriates were only few in numbers. Especially the Counsellor, Mr. Schiffer, took to him, introduced N. to others of the staff and to his family. He was invited to all cocktail parties, met diplomats of other embassies, was invited there as well and it started to be one wonderful place but of the fact that he was going to run out of money. The Egyptian Press Agency went bankrupt, there were only very few articles he was able to sell to German papers and periodicals. N. had to use some of his reserve money to buy himself an evening suit to be properly dressed.

One day having been invited to Mr. Schiffer's home he sat down at the grand piano and played a few popular tunes when Mr. Schiffer got very excited.

"Can you play some German folk songs?" he asked N.

N. answered that he could try.

"Because," continued the Councillor, "we can have a small German choir."

"A choir?"

"Yes. We can invite some of the ex-patriates, we can meet once a week here. And if you ask why? I will tell you. A German choir means we do something cultural. And for that the German Government will have fly in a barrel of beer every week as diplomatic luggage, customs free and all that. We shall have a lovely time."

And so it went. Some six of the expatriates, all working in the building sector working with concrete on the airfield, burly types with rough voices, formed the "choir". They once a week came along, sang two sweet songs and afterwards enjoyed German beer from the barrel. It was great. Unfortunately someone from the Pakistan Unesco office heard about it and invited the "German Choir" to appear at an international function with "Music and Folkdancing".

The venue was the inner court of the Metropol Hotel. Among the audience were some ambassadors with their wives. The German "singers" went on stage after they had a tot of spirits to calm down their stage fright. And off it went. Musically it was a fiasco, the German ambassador silently left. But the Pakistan minister of education presented N. with a diploma of gratitude. Well, it was quite some fun in those days in Karachi.

The waiter of the Sartaj boarding house served tea and cake on a small table in N's room. Only after hearing the waiter's steps on the old wooden staircase, he talked to Kreisel.

"Here we are safe. No hidden microphones."

N's room on the roof had a wonderful mosaic floor of small blue-green tiles. A small balcony had enough space for two chairs and a little table. On a clear day without dust one could see the brown-yellow stony desert of Sindh province. Coming up from the stairs there was a spacious terrace where there was a bathroom. From the terrace one could view innumerable back yards and other flat roof tops.

"I have thought last night and would like to discuss it with you."

"Go ahead," said Kreisel while biting into one of the extremely sweet cakes.

"With the Russians it works well," N. continued, "but we could enlarge."

"How?"

"I can imagine that not only the Russians are interested what we can offer. But there are the Indians who, I think, would like to know what the Americans are building."

Kreisel helped himself to tea and grinned. "Some sort of wholesale?"

"Exactly. If I work it out carefully, it will go well provided I get the material from you."

"No problem on my side. I can get all the plans copied. But the thick volume with all the specifications does exist only once and I shall have to make copies as we go along. It will be only two months in my possession to calculate the weekly work."

"That gives us two months to complete our big business."

"Well that applies to the runways only," Kreisel explained, "but there will be the bunker and ammunition depots. The plans for these I shall get after the two months."

Kreisel got up to go and they parted amiably.

The following afternoon N. entered through a heavy iron gateway across a flagstoned yard of the building on top of which the Indian flag was hoisted.

A young Indian asked him politely to wait in the hall which was refreshingly cool.

N. had asked to see the military attaché. He was led to the first floor into an office where a middle-aged Indian with intelligent eyes was looking at N. and asked him to take a seat.

"What can I do for you?"

"Well, I am going to ask you if you are interested to get the complete technical details including blue prints of the airfields the Americans are building in Pakistan at present."

"Of course we are interested. But at the moment I would like to know your motivation, the choice of our country, and, of course, all about you."

He pressed a button, a servant came in and he ordered tea. He got up from behind his desk, waived to a group of easy chairs -

"Lets sit here and talk."

The tea was served, cigarettes were offered and N. reported in detail about his years in India, showed his letter of introduction which he had obtained from the Indian Information Office in Madras, showed his passport with the Indian visa and declared that he would have to ask for money on delivery of the material handed over.

The attaché put his tea cup down, lit a cigarette.

"I think we can come to an agreement, but first of all I have to see what you can give us."

"Certainly," explained N. "but I cannot deliver all in one go, but always in parts only which I can let you have in the evenings and must have to return it the same night."

"That is O.K. My name is Mehta, I am the councillor. For you I am Uncle. If you phone the embassy you tell whoever answers that you have greetings for Uncle. He then will connect you to me and we can arrange place and time. For the first installment you will meet one of my people at the entrance of the Metro cinema at Bunder Road. He will take you to my office and take you back. And for you we will have to agree to a code name."

"I suggest Mohammed," replied N.

Mr. Mehta smiled: "Quite good because we are in a Muslim country."

He pressed a bell again and gave an order to the servant. Shortly afterwards another Indian, a Punjabi, entered the room.

"Look at his face so that you remember him. He will meet you at the foyer of the cinema shortly before the eight o'clock show."

N. left the embassy in high spirits, waved a motor-rickshaw which took him to the Metropol Hotel.

Now he needed a drink. He went to the bar. A couple of British people sat there and talked about cotton prices. Then he went to the German reading room next door.

"Good that you come," the manager Mr. Konieczki, "I have something for you."

"I hope it is not snakes," N. laughed because once Mr. Konieczki had taken two small snakes out of his pocket. The manager, commander of a submarine during the Second World War, living now in Karachi, married to a Pakistani, had an unusual hobby; He caught snakes on most sundays in the Thar Desert for some German research institutes.

"No snakes today," he said, "but there is the Iraqi military attaché who desperately wants German lessons. My timetable is full. I have recommended you to him and he expects you at four today. He lives at the Metropol."

This sounded good. Konieczki tended to his chores, N. looked at some German newspapers and soon Kreisel walked in.

N. lowered his voice and told him about the Indian. That he expected to have the first delivery tonight. As Kreisel's boarding house was not far away from Bunder Road they agreed to meet at seven.

Fifteen minutes before the start of the evening show the cinemas foyer was filled with a crowd. On the programme was "High Society" and Grace Kelly as well as Louis Armstrong seems to be a hit of the Pakistani cinema goers.

N. was on the lookout for the Punjabi but could not find him in this mass of people.

When he felt a soft touch on his sleeve and he turned, he recognised him and followed him some paces behind. A car was parked in a side lane. N. got in and the driver carefully found his way out of the large number of people, Rickshaws and stalls which could be found in front of every cinema in Pakistan.

From Bunder Road they took the Victoria Street and went straight to Clifton. N. was startled, this was not the way to the embassy. The car went sharply around several corners and came to a stop in front of a grand old villa. N. put his head down when he noticed the glaring lights.

The car stopped at a side entrance. The corridors were simply furnished.

On the first floor he entered an office and found "Uncle" sitting behind an ordinary desk. The room was not decorated for representation but was an ordinary working place.

"Where are we here?" N. asked after greetings were exchanged.

"This is the General Consulate, and this is where I am mostly doing my business. Sit down, please."

The tea was brought in and N. took a large envelope from under his shirt.

Kreisel had given him the plan of the airport with its runways and some pages of specifications.

N. leaned back, enjoyed a cup of Darjeeling tea, smoked a cigarette and waited. Uncle rang the bell and another Indian entered who reminded N. of a student of the school of engineering in Guindy near Madras: A lean face with intelligent eyes behind spectacles.

"Our photographic expert," Uncle introduced him and handed him the material.

When they were alone N. started to discuss the business side. "We have to ask for five thousand Rupees or, preferably, in other currencies such as British pound or dollars, for each delivery." Uncle made a sad face like a carpet seller who was going to haggle.

They finally agreed for two thousand Rupees and two thousand five-hundred dollars.

"I have only one thousand Rupees with me," Uncle said and made a face like a green grocer in Bombay who can't pay his rent, "you get the difference next time."

"Together with the whole sum for the next delivery".

"Of course."

N. signed the receipt and they waited for less than an hour, when the photo expert returned with the papers. Uncle smiled when the expert told him that he was satisfied.

Uncle explained the modalities which were almost the same as with the Russians: An empty street, the car approached slowly, the head lights dimmed N. entered the car quickly, which dashed off, working its way through innumerable streets and lanes and finally landed at the General Consulate.

A number of weeks these deliveries to the satisfaction of Kreisel and N. as well as to the Russians and the Indians as buyers went very well indeed until one night the car of the Russian was followed by another car.

"There is a jeep behind us, could be American," Kuimov said, "keep your head down and jump out at the next bend."

The car moved into a small lane, stopped for a second, N. got out and hid for a moment in an archway. The jeep went after the Russian car, but N. was safe.

He stayed about five minutes in the darkness. The lane was quiet. He decided not to go to Kreisel's boarding house but to find his way to his hotel. He had an envelope with secret material and money under his shirt.

In the main streets he mingled with the crowds, emerging from the late shows of the cinemas, as inconspicuous as he could make himself. He forced himself to walk leisurely and wondered why in the films the fugitives always were running which only would draw attention to them especially in a hot climate where everyone would walk at a very slow pace.

He managed to enter his room and hid the discriminating envelope. His heartbeat calmed down. It took quite some time before he could sleep.

The next day he met Kreisel at the German Reading Room and explained why he did not turn up. Under cover of a newspaper he handed an envelope with half the money to Kreisel. The material he still needed for the evening delivery to Uncle. He had arranged with the Indian for an earlier meeting.

But it was already getting dark when N., dressed in dinner suit, handed over the material.

"Why the change of time?" Uncle wanted to know.

"Because I have an evening invitation tonight at the house of Mr. Kierman of the American Embassy. You know Christmas time is approaching and the invitation says Cocktails and Carols."

"Be careful," advised Uncle, "Mr. Kierman is the CIA agent in station here. He may, casually, ask questions."

"I met him some time ago at the German Embassy where, by the way I have to go tomorrow to meet Mr. Hallstein, the Foreign Affairs Secretary of State. And after tomorrow I have an invitation to meet the Begum Ali Khan."

"Well, you do get around," Uncle smiled. But then he added: "In case it should be necessary for you to leave this country in a hurry, we offer you on any day a courier seat on our Air India plane which always leaves Karachi at noon. The airline officer at the check-in counter will be supplied a photo of yours and will issue travel documents."

"This is very kind of your Government. I hope I do not have to use it."

The Indian car drove N. near the Kierman's home. The material and money was carefully folded in the inner pocket of N's tuxedo. N. held his cocktail glass with the help of a paper napkin to avoid having his finger prints on the glass. You never know, he thought. He reached his hotel by midnight. No questions had been asked at the party. N. was relieved.

A few days later Kuimov gave N. a tiny German Minox camera which was used by intelligence agents during World War 2 and afterwards. The valet of the British ambassador in Ankara had received one to photograph secret documents from the ambassadors safe. The valet, Elyesa Bazna, code-named Cicero, had been paid in counterfeit pound Sterling notes which he did not suspect at that time. He was never caught though and lived up to his death in Istanbul. Kuimov knew about this case and only mentioned, that his payments are not counterfeit.

Kuimov explained the working of the camera and said that it would be wiser to photograph the documents.

"To carry a small film roll is easier than to carry paper documents with you."

N. agreed. Kuimov supplied him with a dozen films and N. was enthusiastic, because Kreisel could always make two films, one for the Russians and one for the Indians.

On a short trip to Quetta N. spend a few days with a Parsi ingenieur stationed there. He had just discovered a large brown coal deposit. N. copied the details and handed them to the trade attaché of the German embassy who was delighted and said that he would hear from them.

In the early days of January 1957 things developed rapidly. It started with a letter from the Pakistani Immigration Office to hand over N's passport for scrutiny. This was suspicious because N. had got only a few months ago the extension of his visa.

He raced to his friend from the Australian High Commission to obtain an entry visum. No problem.

At the last delivery to the Russians he bid farewell, received, among others, a cigarette case with instructions to call on the Soviet Embassy in Jakarta, ask for the First Secretary and offer him a cigarette from this case. That was to be his introduction. N. then told Kuimov that from now on he would have to deal directly with Kreisel. Not a problem.

Then he had his last delivery to the Indians. Uncle had difficulties to have all the money ready. N. trusted him and gave uncle the bank account number of his friend who had moved to Australia, Uncle promised to send five thousand dollars to that account. A cable to his friend in Australia was the final item to be done, apart from getting his air ticket from KLM to Sydney via Bangkok and Manila.

Then he went to his bank, withdrew all the money, obtained quite a number of traveller cheques leaving only some dollars to meet travel expenses.

This was followed by a series of farewell parties at the German Embassy, where Mr. Schiffer told him that he would be contacted by the Embassy there as soon as he had given them his address. Finally his friend Dr. Z. and his family wished him bon voyage. It was a hectic time. N. was glad not to have contacted the Iraqi military attaché who was supposed to meet him.

The last day was busy packing. His original two pieces of luggage developed into five suitcases.

Those were exhausting days with the Pakistani still waiting for his passport.

Fortunately there were no difficulties at the check-in and departure from Karachi airport.

And then N. took off for Australia.

DIVERTISSEMENT

In January 1957 I collected N. from Sydney airport. He was his smiling self but looked lean and exhausted. We drove in my Holden car all the way to Melbourne staying there overnight. Next day N. wanted to register at the German Consulate General. I had told him on the way that I had rented a studio flat for him in Anzac Highway in Adelaide because I was teaching at that time in a high school there and he could give his new address to the Consulate.

I dropped him at his new flat in Adelaide.

That night was taken up less by sleep but by much talking. N. mentioned his affairs with the Russians only sparingly and not in full detail. I did not force him to reveal more but I knew he would explain when he felt like it.

"And what are your plans now?" I asked him.

"I don't really know it. All I need now is a long rest to digest it all", he answered, "I need to re-do myself.

"By the way your money has arrived from some company in Delhi."

"I was right to trust Uncle," N. smiled.

I offered him to introduce him to the Czech expatriate club. "You will find some interesting people there. There is a German club too, but it is somewhat dull there and the members seem to be more Australian than the Australian themselves. You find that often with new convertites. And then you should do some travelling, to Tasmania and the Northern territories. This should give you some impressions of the variety of Australia which is not a country but a continent."

"Give me some time, and I shall certainly do it," N. replied. I left him at that giving him my phone number and drove to my own flat.

AUSTRALIA 1957

When N. left the plane in Sydney he, as usual, sniffed to take in the smell of this, for him, new country. He found that Australia smelt of Eucalyptus, quite different from Egypt, India and Pakistan, and quite pleasant too.

When his friend left him in his flat in Adelaide he was pleased: bedroom, lounge, kitchenette and bath, all small but tastefully furnished.

So he started unpacking his books, typewriter, carpets from Pakistan, personal things to make it homely.

It was a nice flat, very near the sea and his friend's house not too far away.

In the morning he went to a bank, opened an account using his traveller cheques and the money from India which his friend had given him. It was altogether enough to live reasonably well for a year or two. He did some shopping and admired the wonderfully laid out parks.

The newspapers were full of the witch-hunt against Soviet spies in Australia, having arrested one or two with the help of the CIA.

Being eager to meet people and with introductions arranged by his friend N. made some helpful contacts within a few weeks.

Professor Thompson invited N. to accompany him to an Aboriginal Reserve in Arnhem Land in the barren part of north Australia. There N. met with people who still lived almost in the stone-age. They ate raw lizards, slurped from puddles of rare rain water like dogs, and it was a feast for the whole tribe when they caught one of those ferocious crocodiles which they buried on hot stones in a dug-out pit for a few days until they were cooked, sort of.

But most fascinating was their philosophy of life which was not at all neolithic.

What do we humans want, being members of all creatures in this world?

Is it happiness, satisfaction and peace? The Australian Aborigines have found the ideal solution.

"What is the aim of your people in life?" he asked the head-man of the Nullangi tribe.

"Very easy" answered the tribal chief laughingly, "all people full a'tummy, hunting and rain plenty, plenty."

And when N. inquired about the miracle of death and birth, he just said: "All dream."

It is quite interesting to ponder about this dream philosophy of people who do not know the concept of time. Actually it is really insignificant to know or not to know how the universe was created, if at all, and by whom or by what. Knowledge or not knowledge may make man happier on the surface, but it also makes us to sheep. All our problems are related to our concept of time.

To solve these problems one should remove oneself from the fetters of time. If people hear these thoughts they, at once, will say that they have no time to think about it, N. was reflecting.

The western people whose mind has created the concept of time, have no time to free themselves of it.

How different the Asians. Their minds are slowly digesting the western concept and have the time to do so. One cannot free oneself of something which one does not have.

These thoughts brought N. immediately to Krishnamurti who spoke to N. in India not to think of past and future but to live in the present, from moment to moment.

And now he hears more or less the same from Australian Aborigines that past and future, death and birth belong to dreamland.

Why have the white conquerors never studied the native people, their peaceful attitude, their thoughts, their holy sites - like Ayer's Rock in Central Australia, their caves in the Blue Mountains in the east with their paintings dating back some thousands years?

Instead they introduced alcohol like the settlers did with Red Indians in America.

On another occasion he met the director of the Adult Education Department who arranged for N. to give travel talks on Egypt, India and Pakistan .

He made friends with Jan, a Czech emigré and his family. There were parties with all kinds of people and lively discussions.

He visited a small town in Tasmania where he experienced another aspect of life in Australia.

Smithton has an official population of 700 but it is the seat of the municipality and the largest town in the extreme northwest of Tasmania.

Through Smithton by rail, highway and ship timber and livestock are sent to other parts of the state and the mainland, rich, clannish in the way isolated towns are with two churches, many milk-bars with a traffic light on the main street to slow down the slow moving traffic, with a public library, a masonic lodge, a man's club and the town hall where they show weekly pictures, occasional pseudo cultural events dragged in by a hopeful dramatic club and now and then grim little concerts given by one of the religious groups. And, of course, balls and dances.

There is a primary school and a high school, a town police force of three, a voluntary fire brigade. Like other small towns its street plan is the result neither of chance or thought but natural development.

Along the rail road tracks are loading pens, industrial buildings, a canning factory, a butter factory and above all a number of timber mills. And last not least one hotel with a lively much frequented pub run by Ryan an Irishman with his family. That is where N. stayed and he liked the pub. He played popular tunes on the old piano and all joined in.

As a newcomer he at once was invited by a wealthy mill owner and his family on their weekly parties being glad to see a new face with interesting tales to tell about far away exotic countries.

Slowly N. regained his old self but for one thing: No newspaper contracts, not even on a freelance basis. His journalistic career seems to have ended.

An old friend in Germany having heard of N's talks on countries visited arranged to give talks in Nigeria and Ghana, where he had connections.

Jan and his German friend in Adelaide persuaded him to take it and suggested that N. should inform himself on West African history to understand the African mentality better.

Books were bought, N. studied emsily and his lack of African issues were fading. Visas were entering his passport and he was looking for airlines to take him there which was not so easy on account of the international embargo to pass South Africa where the Apartheid policy had climbed high. To reach Nigeria he had to go by Qantas from Sydney to Rome, from there by Egypt Air to Cairo, using Ghana Airways to Nigeria for a short stop to go on from Lagos to Accra. And all that for about a week's stay.

With just one small suitcase he arrived at Lagos airport and after passport control was whisked away to a small room. His case was emptied, his books and papers were scrutinised thoroughly, he had to strip until he stood naked surrounded by fierce looking armed guards.

"Can anyone tell me what is going on?" N. managed to shout.

"Keep quiet," came the answer from an officer recognizable by his many stars on his shoulder.

N. kept quiet. His clothes were searched and, finding nothing, he was told to dress. His belongings were put back into the suitcase. The officer returned his passport to him.

"You are declared persona non grata. You are permitted to stay one night at the airport hotel. You are not to leave the room until tomorrow morning to take the first plane to Accra."

N. was taken by guards to the Hotel adjacent to the airport where he got a meal. He was furious but thought it better not to complain or ask for an explanation. It could make matters worse.

Looking out of the window he noticed below a small river surrounded by lush foliage and a crocodile swimming lazily. Much safer than iron bars or barbed wire, he considered.

Next morning a guard accompanied him to the airport to board the plane of Ghana Airways. Two hours later he landed in Accra. Like in Lagos the air smelled of humidity and dust.

N. went straight to the German embassy and told his story. The official felt for him but could not do anything.

"It is your surname," he said, "there is an English mercenary who trains rebels in the North, who has the same surname. So it must be a case of mistaken identity. They may have taken you for a relative."

With the help of the embassy official N. found a pleasant bungalow hotel on the beach outside the bustling city of Accra. He contacted the University in Kumasi and was told that he would be collected in two days at noon.

And punctually a car drove up, N. got in and they, after a quick lunch, set off for Kumasi the provincial capital of Ashanti-Land.

It was a wonderful six hour drive on a passable road through cacao fields, small hamlets and villages, along rivers and tropical forests. They paused for refuelling, some snacks and tea. The driver, a muscular proud Ashanti talked about his country, the governor, the King of Ashanti-Land. N. was looking forward to come to know West Africa.

Kumasi appeared to be a lovely town with a lively market place, with friendly people, the women dressed in colourful robes of Kente cloth, smiling men and, above all, a most modern University compound nicely laid out surrounded by lush foliage and high palm trees.

Dr. Agyeman, the regional director of education, received N. warmly, showed him the guesthouse next to his own. The meals he shared with the family. He was introduced to the staff of the university in the main building. N. was very pleased with all he saw. But after the long trip he bade Good Night early and settled down in the guest house, read for some time, but somehow he could not find sleep. He had kept the windows, protected by fly screens, open and the sound of the surrounding bushes and palm trees, a soft mild breeze, the humming of insects, the cawing of night birds, the pitter-patter of tiny monkey feet on the tin roof and the distant sound of drums kept him awake.

A real African Night. He switched off the lamp, listened and found that life can be wonderful provided one does not get weak. Next morning, after breakfast he walked to the lecture hall and spoke to a hundred students about strange Asian countries, about their history, their way of life, their attitudes which, after all, are not very different from theirs. This was followed in the afternoon by a question-and-answer session.

It was, N. thought, a successful debut. The students were quite enthusiastic and the director presented N. with a lovely scarf of the finely woven and colourful Kente cloth.

Another day of rest and he received his return ticket. This time a small DC 3 of Ghana Airways took him to Accra where he boarded the Russian Aeroflot plane on a bumpy flight to Cairo for a stop-over. N. used the time to drive to Gizeh to Heli's house but found that she had sold it and moved to Alexandria. BOAC carried him to Sydney where Ansett Airways brought him safely to Adelaide, on a warm day of October, 1958.

In his flat he found some letters waiting for him.

Among the mail was a postcard showing a Siberian scene with birch trees and ornate wooden houses, postmarked Gaczyna, Soviet Union, with only one sentence written: "Wish you were here", signed Kreisel.

Now, how on earth knew anyone in the Soviet Union his address in Australia? Was it Kuimov who had alerted the Russian Embassy in Canberra? Who had traced him to Adelaide? It was most embarrassing. Another, very official letter from the Ministry of Commerce in Germany containing a contract to write economic reports on Australia payable with one Deutschmark per line. This was preposterous, N. thought and wrote at once an answering letter refusing this contract because it could be misinterpreted by the Australian Government. He enclosed the contract and would post it tomorrow.

Next day late morning the bell rang in N.'s apartment. Three men were at the door when N. opened. Politely one of them asked whether he was N.

"I am and who are you?" N. asked.

They showed little official cards with their fotos laminated in small leatherbound wallets.

"I am Bill Roper, special agent from security of the Melbourne office.

And these are Mr. Roberts and Mr. Jarvis from our Adelaide bureau."

"Please come in."

They went into the living room, N. invited them to take a seat and offered a drink which they refused.

"And what can I do for you?"

"Quite a lot," Bill Roper said and politely carried on "you have received your mail?"

"Yes, I have."

"We are interested about two things. First the contract with the German Ministry of Commerce -"

"So you have opened the letter?" N. interrupted.

"Of course, we thought it necessary."

"Then you can rest in peace," N. remarked and showed him the letter refusing the contract. "And you can post it, if you don't mind."

They were satisfied .

"But now to the postcard you received from the Soviet Union."

"I was asking myself," explained N.," why they wrote to me and especially how they come to know my address here."

"Quite right, we did too," Roper agreed, "do you know the name Kreisel? It was signed by him."

N. hesitated a few seconds, then answered "Yes".

"We assume that you are working for the KGB." Roper stated.

"No. I never worked for the KGB," N. replied truthfully.

"Well, we know otherwise," Jarvis butted in.

"Then provide the evidence," N. demanded.

"For one, you admitted to know this man Kreisel. For another you received a postcard from him, postmarked Gaczyn."

"So what?"

"Then we shall inform you about Gaczyn," Roper lectured, "Gaczyn is one of nine top-secret establishments of the KGB in the Soviet Union to train future agents specially used in English speaking countries. Kreisel must have been recruited by them in Pakistan, when you were there as we know. Who is Kreisel and what did he do?"

"He was an overseer of a work-team building airfields for American companies, as far as I know." N. replied.

"Very good," Roper stated, "now we have to ask you how you fitted into this. The USA give military aid to Pakistan. They give the contract to an American building company who, in turn, engage a man named Kreisel to oversee this job, who seems to be now in the Soviet Union at the top-secret spy school in Gaczny. We think that you are the link between Kreisel's job and the Russians in Karachi, isn't it?"

N. did some fast thinking.

"If it is so," he replied, "why are you after me? I am not doing anything wrong in Australia?"

"No, you do not do anything wrong yet. But maybe the Soviets send you here? We have to be careful. Our British colleagues have caught a Mr. Osborne recently who lived ten years in Australia, built up a prospering Import and Export company while also building up a centre of commercial espionage."

"I do understand your concern," N. said.

"We want to know with whom you had dealings in the Soviet embassy in Karachi. We know that you had a number of contacts in various embassies there," Jarvis said just a bit demanding.

N. had read about the system of interrogation, the technique using one nice and polite person and one bad, tough one. Roper was the decent chap, Jarvis the hard one. The third never said anything. Was he the boss?

N. wanted to avoid lengthy interrogations. On the other hand they could not persecute him on anything in Australia. So he gave in and told them.

Roper asked for details, Jarvis took notes. When N. mentioned the cigarette case to be used when making contact in Jakarta, they asked for it promising to hand it back to him.

"That, for the time being is all," Roper concluded in a satisfactory and soft voice, "for the moment we request you not to leave town, we shall be back in a few days."

"You are not arresting me?"

"Why should we?" he smiled and all three left.

N. went into the kitchen and drank a large whisky.

66

The same afternoon he consulted his German and Czech friends. They both concluded that N. did the right thing to reveal his Pakistan activities.

"In Pakistan you stuck your neck out," Jan remarked.

"That's what necks are for," countered N., "a grasp of essentials and a capacity for survival are the two qualities needed."

"You seem to have both of them," Jan stated.

N. was careful not to mention the Indian connection. Although appreciating that his friends took his revelation as a matter of fact and without any judgement, he did not want to burden them unduly.

So the days passed by. N. did much walking in Adelaide's beautiful, well kept park, spent much time in his friend's house in Outer Harbour near the beach or with Jan and his family playing cards and having political discussions.

A week later, end of October, Roper was back, this time alone.

"You were right not to have had contacts with the KGB," he told N. "we checked on Kuimov and indeed he is a GRU man, military intelligence. We have decided you to go to Jakarta to make contact with the military intelligence officer of the Soviet embassy there as Kuimov had told you. Here, by the way, is your cigarette case which obviously is your means of identification.

We pay for the air fare, accommodation and some travel expenses. You are to leave on 21 January next year and return on 23rd January. You take your press cards with you to cut out any interest from Indonesian intelligence."

"That means that, in effect, I am working now for Australian Counter Intelligence?" N. asked.

Roper smiled.

"In a way," he said, "but we are taking the risk. Mr. Jarvis and Mr. Roberts will see you prior to your departure, hand you tickets and money. You gave them quite some time following you around your walks in Adelaide."

The brandnew BOAC turbo-jet took off in time. There were only four passengers on board of this solely first class plane. Male and female attendants were in the majority and spoiled the travellers serving drinks, snacks, three course meals and even cigarettes. N. had never before such a wonderful time flying.

Jakarta airport had a very similar smell as India: Sweet flowers and that particular fragrance of bushes and trees after a monsoon rain.

A hotel was found quickly followed by an evening stroll through crowded streets full of shops, restaurants, food stalls, fruit and vegetable vendors and spices in this silky mildness only found in the tropics. He bought a street map and a lovely carving of a gracefully praying woman.

The next morning a taxi brought him to the Japanese embassy only a block away from the Soviet embassy, which he covered on foot. He entered and asked for the military attaché. He was led to a comfortably furnished room. The attaché entered and N. offered him a cigarette. The attaché smiled, acknowledged and replied: "Have one of mine." With this contact was established.

He explained that there was a change of plans though. Intelligence business in Australia was now assigned to the embassy in Wellington.

So N. would have to go to New Zealand. He handed N. one thousand US dollars to cover his expenses coming here, shook his hand and escorted him to the entrance hall.

N. had one full day on his own, bought some newspapers printed in English and learned that Senator MacCarthy and his followers were still hunting down Communists. Laughing to himself he thought that the US Senator should just take a look into the Moscow telephone directory and he would find millions.

N. spent the time wandering around.

On the 23rd he arrived in Sydney by Qantas and in the evening landed in Adelaide.

Roper came the next day to the flat and N. reported. N. thought it wise to hand over the money he had received. Roper appreciated the gesture, gave N. his telephone number in Melbourne. They parted amiably.

N. unpacked his Indonesian souvenir and the praying woman found a nice place in his bookshelf.

On 5th May 1959 N. boarded a Qantas plane to Wellington. A few seats behind him Bill Roper and Jarvis were sitting. It was agreed that they would not know each other either on the flight or in Wellington. Roper would contact him in the hotel room.

The talk in the room developed into a briefing of how to go about, what to say, not to take any notes but to memorize what he was told. N. suggested to use a mini-microphone and a mini-recorder, but Roper dismissed it as the Russians may use electronic detectors.

N. followed the same procedure as in Jakarta. A taxi brought him a block before the embassy. Entering the embassy he asked for the military attaché. The diplomat entered the waiting room pretending not to know N., he ignored the identity cigarette case and simply said "You must be mistaken. I have to ask you to leave."

N. left and met a disappointed Roper in the hotel room. N. repeated several times his visit and the encounter.

"There must have been a leak," N. said.

"It seems to be like that," Roper agreed.

"It could have been that they found out that they saw you seeing me in Adelaide and they have been on the lookout either following you or watching me." N. suggested.

Roper and his colleague made a sour face and did not answer. They took the next plane back to Australia.

For N. that ended the Soviet connection, as far as he was concerned.

"As far as we are concerned, we have to continue observing you as long as you are in Australia," Roper commented and added: "Let us know when you are leaving Australia."

It was about this time that N. had another creative phase: He discovered painting.

Ivan Strasek, another Czech emigré and an established art dealer helped him along. He arranged exhibitions later even at the Royal South Australian Society of Art open-air exhibition in Adelaide's wonderful park. Besides coming to know new people he even sold quite a number of his works, was invited to parties and thus recovered his old optimistic self.

These parties - well. "His vision of memories was shut off by barriers of fleshy faces, arms, bosoms, chins and tuxedos. The bark and chirrup of human voices manufacturing words which created the illusion of intelligent existence." There were the Woolcombes, the Bakes, the Stymes from Melbourne who bought two paintings, the Pursers, the friendly Rombouts, the Harrisons, the Noyes who owned the Coffee Lounge in Adelaide, some he gave away to his friend Jan L., and many more.

N. liked the Australian way of invitations to informal parties by phone "Tomorrow at eight at the Parkins. Gents a bottle, ladies a basket." Which means that the men brought their drinks, usually good Australian wine, the ladies snacks, salads, cakes.

And women? Wanda, Elizabeth, Heather?

Well, there are crossroads. One separates, perhaps meets again if one is there at the right hour, walks part of the way together, "Ships that pass o'nights." When was the last time in Australia N. had a date that didn't last long? N. always ignored any comments on his love life: "A kiss is just a kiss" he would hum the Casablanca song.

After some years went by, N. wrote a satirical story about the frequent strikes by dockworkers in Australia. Funnily enough they always striked on days when there was to be a dog race or other sporting events which always worked out that it resulted in gaining a long weekend.

He sent this article to the German magazine DER SPIEGEL. They did not publish it but sent a letter from the editor Dr. D. Wild asking if N. would go on a free-lance basis to Uganda to investigate why there are so many Israeli experts advising and training Special units of the Ugandan army.

N. at once forgot his previous lethargy and felt that new adventures, new peoples and places are waiting for him, and that there were possibilities to find back to journalism.

DIVERTISSEMENT

Prior to leaving for Uganda I and his Czech friend Jan were the main contacts with N. It took him some time to overcome his lack of journalistic work as well as the exciting times left behind him. He at times, was depressed and finally started to paint.

He discovered composition, colour values, techniques - and his results were quite good.

It is a well known fact that some people have the most creative phase when they are unhappy. Think of painters, of composers, of writers - they created the finest works of art when they were struggling with either poverty or depression or both.

But as long as his funds allowed him to live in Australia he was also satisfied with hammering on his typewriter and discovering writing as apart from reporting. And his stories were good as well.

"I should have done this or that, the fact is that according to my way of living and my attitude considering the circumstances, all could not have been happening differently," he told me before he left, vital as ever, for Uganda.

UGANDA 1966

Having notified Roper who appeared glad that N. was leaving, having paid taxes N., now 42 years old, booked a passage on the Ellinis of the Greek Chandris Line from Melbourne to Piräus-Athens. He looked forward to this journey by sea not alone for the reason of not having to pay excess luggage, which had grown considerably, as he would have done going by air.

He enjoyed every day, the stop at Colombo where there was time to go on land to have tea at the Taprobane Hotel, the short stop at Aden where British troops patrolled the streets, the leisurely way the big ship made her way through the Suez Canal and, finally, the arrival in Greece.

He had made a number of friends on board, especially a Dutch couple with whom he spent a lovely time in Athens.

N. had booked a cabin on a freighter bound for Mombassa. Once there he went with all his luggage by train via Nairobi to Kampala, when he finally arrived in March 1966.

There had been no airport where he could smell the air of his new country.

The trip on this slow moving old fashioned train, a miniature version of the legendary Orient Express, with its panelled compartments, beautiful art déco table lamps in the mahagony walled dining car, he could make out the fragrance when he opened a window: the dry and red earth in Kenya and later, reaching Uganda, lush tropical foliage mixed with the smell of earth. It was different, but he liked it.

So far he only had a scant knowledge of Uganda. But as Churchill had once said, that Uganda is the pearl of Africa, he trusted his words and only wondered why the British never made it a colony but a protectorate.

You get knowledge only partially from books, that means from others, N. thought. Real knowledge you get from experience whether it is secular or spiritual experience. Of course, your upbringing, your education play a part in the process of developing this urge to direct experience as opposed to blind acceptance what you have been taught.

N. liked experiencing wherever he went.

He rented a comfortable bungalow on a small hill outside Kampala and bought a second-hand small car, a Beatle which had seen better days but it would do nicely. The Sikh who sold him the car and owned a service station advised him never to leave the car unattended during the night.

Thieves are keen to steal the tyres and windscreen wipers. Fortunately, N's house had a garage.

Just below the hill there was a small village with little shambas where people had chicken, a few coffee trees and grew vegetables. In the night, from far away, drums could be heard, - Africa like in old stories.

What fascinated N. at first was this amazing nature of the land. This abundance of beauty under the equator and the pleasant climate due to the altitude of 1200 meters.

N. admired the frangipani in front of his bedroom window, the delicate white flowers with golden centres flowering on the leafless tree and distributing a strong but sweet fragrance.

He went for a short excursion to Lake Nabugabu through alleys of beautiful flamboyant trees covered in brilliant deep red blossoms like flames. He passed small shambas with papayas. Their fruit being a delicious treat. At the lake he was met by hords of large-sized white butterflies and cumbersome looking pelicans with their long beaks and large sacks beneath. They stood there together like old wise men gossiping. Eventually they, with great effort, got into the air, and lazily flew away, perhaps they did not like the smell or sound of N's beatle.

When, after the daily morning shower, the wind dropped and it got damp but refreshing one or two crowned cranes paid a visit to N's garden and he was stunned by their elegant royal deportment. And, during the night, he had company of a number of agile geckos chasing each other on the ceiling and keeping the rooms free of flies and mosquitos.

This was one part of Uganda, of Africa, which N. admired, fascinated by this colourful nature: The world of plants and animals. It was a small world bounded by the sun, the moon and daily rain showers.

The other world - and that was why he had fled it - was the smoke filled pubs, the corridors and waiting rooms of government offices, of laughing and sorrowful, of busy and powerful, of kind and serious people.

It started with N. registering at the German embassy. Mr. Beck, the 1st Secretary, received him friendly and gave him helpful advice whom to meet and where.

"Uganda had after independence still teething troubles," he told N., "there are too many tribes who have their idea of freedom and are not at all eager to accept what is called a unified nation."

"So President Obote has quite some task waiting for him," N. remarked.

"Well, he tries his best."

"In the North and Northwest live the Acholi and the Toro, who are mainly Muslim, in the Northeast are the poorer Karamajong who are not Bantu but Nilothic-hamitic. Anywhere are tribes who are prone to take to arms," Mr. Beck explained.

"I thought Mutesa II, the Kabaka or king ruled the country," N. threw in.

"He was, he was the king of the Muganda, the largest Bantu tribe. They are also the most educated people having been brought up by the many missionary schools. Obote was Prime Minister under him but, with the help of the army and the police made himself President. Mutesa went into exile to London where he is known in all the fashionable nightclubs."

"There is still a state of emergency in Uganda as I had to have a permit for my short trip to Lake Nagugabu," N. mentioned.

" Of course," Mr. Beck answered in the affirmative, "but it is well handled. All in all the ministries and other Government offices down to the smallest township are efficient in all their dealings."

"My queries regarding the Israelis -"

"Everybody knows about them," Mr. Beck laughed, "but you will run up against a wall. If you want precise information you better leave it aside for the time being and first concentrate on reports where you can be sure to have support from the officials concerned. Try subjects like education, health care, economies and definitely tourism, the game reserves. They will help you. If they have proof that you are positively interested in Uganda, they may come forward about the Israelis."

With this advice, N. started to work. He contacted the German monthly magazine "Afrika Heute" (Africa today), and very soon he had to supply a large monthly column.

He contacted schools, the university, medical officers, he visited country clubs and game reserves, met a great number of interesting people and felt good in his old job as roving journalist. But he missed the thrill, the excitement as he had experienced before.

Dr. Sewali, a medical practitioner, a Bantu with a finely chiselled face, a Christian although with two wives, a conservative follower of the exiled Kabaka and, therefore, disliking Obote and the ruling party, became a very good friend of N. On politics they used to speak in soft voices only.

On the other hand, Dr. Kiwanuka, a principal education officer, a staunch follower of Obote's party, opened many doors for him.

In the game reserve at Mweya Lodge and the majestic Murchison Falls, N. was delighted to drive in the warden's jeep to observe elephants, zebras, gazelles, lions, leopards, hippos. That was excitement of a different kind. Especially when, at Meya Lodge, he refused to sleep in the hotel, but preferred to stay in a primitive one-room hut without electricity. At night the hut was surrounded by tapping feet, by gnarling and snarling noises. In the middle of the night he had to go to the toilet, which was about 30 meters away. He lit the oil lamp and carefully opened the creaking door. The noises stopped when he held the lamp outside. A huge elephant trotted away in disgust after he took his trunk out of the rubbish bin.

Not far from Mweya Lodge he went, via Kasese, to the Blue Mountain area bordering the Kongo. He wanted to meet the Pygmies. Leaving the car behind he and an interpreter went on a jungle path to a small clearing when he came across a small group of pygmies who were busy building temporary huts of branches. The elderly chief, reaching up to N's shoulders, was very happy to see the white man but asked if he could return "when the moon was half", meaning in two weeks. They exchanged some gifts and the chief asked N. to bring, on his return, a book. N. was most astonished but promised to do so.

N. had to go anyway for a week or so to the Murchison Falls in the North.

In Murchison Falls Lodge he was invited by the game warden to come along chasing poachers in the savanna north of Kulu who had been reported to go after rhinos. N. readily accepted. They went in an open truck with five armed wardens first over sand pits later across the grass land. An hour or two they came across some rhinos who at once charged the vehicle.

"Hold on," the warden shouted and went like a rabbit zig-zagging to escape the angry beasts. Rhinos are ferocious when disturbed and are able to smash a truck to pieces due to their weight. After several attempts they gave up. The whining engine may have given them a momentary shock.

Much later they came towards a group of men, squatting under an acacia tree. The jeep halted, the wardens jumped out with their rifles pointing at them, ready to shoot should the men grab to their rifles.

The wardens confiscated their rifles and let them go. No arrests could be made, there was no evidence of a killed rhino nearby.

Back in Kasese N. was searching for a suitable book to give to the pygmy. He wondered what kind of book he could find as he could neither read nor write. Finally, in Kasese's only bookstall, he found a "childrens" book with many coloured pictures of the animals of the jungle.

Another week later he went with the interpreter back to the jungle. After some searching they found the clan and N. presented the book to the chief. He looked at it, studied the animals most of which he knew, smiled and said (through the interpreter): "Now I have a book. I am a great chief. A book is the magic of the white man."

N. was very moved and never should forget this encounter. Indeed, he thought, any good book can be magic.

Later on, back in Kampala, N. decided to walk right into the lion's den, but to approach his queries in a round-about way when he finally met with the press attaché of the Israeli Embassy.

"Israel has certain ties with Uganda," he started off, "it could have gone back to 1903 -"

"1903?" the attaché asked surprised.

"Yes" replied N., "in 1903 Joseph Chamberlain, at that time Prime Minister of Great Britain had been asked by Theodore Herzl on behalf of the Zionists for support in obtaining a colonisation charter for the Sinai Peninsula. Chamberlain was not able to persuade the British authorities in Egypt but he saw the Jews as enterprising agents of colonisation, so he offered them Uganda as a substitute for Palestine."

"This idea of 1903 never was realized. Uganda simply was not the land of our ancestors." remarked the attaché, "we are living now, the situations are different -"

"- but you sent military advisors from Israel to Uganda, that is a factual situation. Why?" N. interrupted.

"I have no knowledge of that, but why should a country not help another country which had a few years ago become independent and wants to be advised to be assisted to obtain its freedom?"

"No country in the world today acts benevolently, out of compassion. There must be very hard reasons for it: Payment, economic or supporting Israel in international fora such as the United Nations.

"One hand takes, the other has to give in return -" N. threw in. The attaché smiled. "What do you really want?" he asked.

"I like to have details about these advisors, what precisely are their objectives, which are the special training programmes, who are the Uganda's special units which are to be trained, etc., etc."

"All this is beyond my knowledge. Our discussion was quite interesting but leads us nowhere. I don't recall that I admitted even, that there are Israeli advisors in Uganda." the attaché said politely but firmly.

He got up, so did N.

This was the wall Mr. Beck from the German embassy had spoken of, N. thought and left.

That took care of his hopes ever to write for DER SPIEGEL.

At the Ministry of Commerce he interviewed the Deputy Minister, Mr. Charles Alai. Besides the exploitation of Copper (in the hands of US firms) and raw coffee (which were sold via the local Coffee Board to the Coffee Board in London) it was interesting to note that much of export was done through barter. N. learned that coffee was collected from plantations, small farms and even from tiny individual shambas with their one or two coffee trees. He came to know all about the Robusta and Arabica sorts. The trouble was that coffee prices are not fixed, so that no regular income could be guaranteed.

Another useful meeting N. had with a Turkish entrepreneur who visited Uganda and, in the course of their conversation, asked N. to come to Turkey to work for him. N. kept it in his mind as he never knew what may happen.

So far he did not do badly and even felt satisfaction being in this country with its undiscribely wonderful nature. Each sunset was a revelation. Satisfaction up to a point because the unsettled political situation reminded him to keep his flexibility alert for action at a moment's notice.

As far as social life was concerned, N. loved the improvised parties no, not parties, but gatherings - under a velvet-black sky with millions of bright stars at the garden of the Apollo hotel. He went there with some people he knew, they were joined by friends and friends of friends. All of them well educated, some newspaper people, students and professionals. It was what is called a jolly good crowd, full of laughter and hilarious situations, washing it down with locally brewed beer and locally made Warangi, a drink made from bananas with a highly potent alcoholic content.

Nobody ever got drunk. It was noisy but of cheerful nature. Politics were tabu.

They were merry despite the state of emergency outside the hotel compound. Or because of it?

Does there exist a dividing line between what you fearfully feel inside and between how you want to appear to others? N. thought. Is the easy-going not part of the African mentality and suitable for the purpose of hiding the fears deep down?

But, come to think of it, is it only African mentality?

One night shortly before Christmas after two years in Uganda, N's friend, Dr. Sewali carefully approached him bringing disturbing news.

The struggle of power which also involves big money and often ruthless behaviour usually carried out by big men, such as Idi Amin, who started as a lance corporal with the British Army's Uganda Rifles, which saw action in the Second World War in North Africa. He ended up in the Uganda Army as a selfmade general and now being appointed by Obote as Chief of the armed forces.

"This is very suspicious," Dr. Sewali said, "Up to now the army stands behind Obote, but Amin is liked by the troops, they even call him Dada, which means father. His aim is to throw out all the Indians as they are controlling economy, they own cotton mills, factories, big and small shops everywhere in the country. After that he plans to do the same with all white people who have dealings with or work in Uganda.

He is brutal and cruel and prone any time to take over from Obote.

"When do you think it will happen?" N. asked.

"My contacts who are usually well informed speak of weeks but possibly a few months."

Dr. Sewali looked very sad and N. felt the same sadness, because both loved Uganda.

N. acted quickly. He posted his last articles and sent a cable to the Turkish tourist entrepreneur, that he would like to talk to him in Istanbul in a few days, packed his belongings, sold his car, paid some bills, said Good Bye only to his dear friend, bought a ticket to Istanbul via Athens.

He reached Istanbul on 2nd of January.

TURKEY 1968

How did Istanbul Airport smell? N. was not quite sure, it seemed to be a mixture of air pollution caused by the many cars and trucks and a whiff of spices from the bazaar.

In any case it was bitterly cold.

At the hotel he quickly changed into warmer clothes. The discussion with the tourist manager went very well. He designed N. to one of his many branches in Bursa.

"You will like Bursa, it is called Yeshil Bursa, the Green Bursa, and is the first capital of the Ottoman Empire. You will be the guide for the many European tourists. Mr. Ali, the manager of the branch will assist you in any way. This appointment is considered to be a start for you."

N. looked forward to this opportunity, the new challenge, the new experience, this new life.

Two days later he reached Bursa, going by ferry to Yalova, from there by small pick-up truck (his luggage!!) to the town below the snow covered Ulu Dag, the Big Mountain.

It was even colder than Istanbul, but there was no snow in and around the town.

Seldom has N. seen such a lovely and charming oriental place with all these splendid mosques, stately mausoleums - all covered with greencoloured tiles, with gardens and parks nearly being drowned in the green foliage of cypress's, the brightly coloured tiled houses, the small lanes, the squares with ornamental fountains. He asked himself how long this wonderful impression would last, considering the development of these modern times.

Mr. Ali put him up in a modern penthouse with a terrace at least twice the size of the little rooms from where he overlooked the town right opposite the Green Mosque.

Ali took him by car to the places the tourist have to see on their day excursion according to the programme, left him with leaflets, historical facts and figures and then told him the coach will collect him early morning to the airport to receive a group of British tourists. So work started right away. N. used the rest of the day and parts of the night studying to be ready for his first assignment. Surprisingly, it went better than he had thought. N. was flexible enough to play the role of a well versed tour guide, showing his group the usual sights like the mausoleum of Sultan Osman, the founder of Bursa, the Ulu Cami, the Great Mosque, the Yeshil Cami, the Green Mosque, the old public baths, the Hamams, founded by Greeks and Romans with their wonderful marble pools and, of course, the large bazaar along the Tuzparasi Caddesi.

At the end of the tour he had a novel experience: He received tips. He shared them with the coach driver. The thankful driver having had, for the first time, a tourguide who shared tips with him, advised N. to walk to the bazaar in the evening to collect his commissions from the shop owners. N. did not hesitate and, indeed, the shop owners gave what was his due. Orient in practice, N. thought.

And so it went on. N. noticed that the tourists who came for this excursion to Bursa were not those who came for entertainment, but those who came were genuinely interested in history, archaeology, culture which suited N. fine. There were large groups of Dutch, British and Germans, smaller groups and indi-viduals from France which were taken by taxis.

Lunch was always included in the programme which were taken at Iskander's, a restaurant famous for its special Kebab, the recipe N. noted down for future reference: Very thinly sliced fried mutton put on round flat dough cake, covered by a rich home-made tomato sauce with garlic and topped by ice-cold rich yogurt: A feast for the roof of one's mouth.

The headlines in the newspapers reported that Idi Amin had been appointed Chief of Staff of the Ugandan armed forces by Obote.

This, N. was sure, was Amin's first step to his aim to seize total power.

N. felt an overwhelming sadness thinking of his friends and of the whole country.

More and more German groups with their own tour leaders came to Bursa during the Spring months. The tour leaders were obliged to use local tour guides, and N. was kept quite busy.

One day, after having observed N's work including how he dealt with individual wishes on previous visits one particular tour leader approached him during the lunch break. Although not a Muslim, he was called Mustafa by everyone.

"I have told my boss of your work here and he would like to interview you. He has a big company with over ten coaches and wants to expand his programmes beyond European destinations. You have been to Asia. Would you like to be tour leader and guide developing routes as far as India?"

India by overland route? N. was delighted.

"You can join our group in Istanbul and come to Germany. I shall be back in two weeks."

N. asked Ali for a week's leave and got it. Ali was not too happy as the season had just started.

In two week's time N. went with Mustafa via Istanbul to Munich. In a small town near Munich N. met with Mr. Holter the owner of this enterprise. He admired the large compound with huge garages for the long Mercedes coaches, the own servicing station, the spacious offices and a guest house where N. could stay overnight. They had a lengthy conversation at the end of which N. signed a contract, starting in September. His salary was very satisfactory, he was given a small flat in the town. For first tour, meant as a training, he was given a tour to Greece to learn the know-how from one of Holter's long-standing guides. After that he was given five tours to Great Britain and Ireland, lasting 27 days each, then one tour to Persia, lasting 37 days and two coaches, the second one with Mustafa, to India, lasting 51 days. The tourists would fly back from Bombay, four days rest while the coaches had to be serviced, the new groups come by air and returned by coaches to Germany.

N. accepted this challenge full-heartedly.

Back in Bursa he told Ali of his future plans, gave the obligatory three month's notice.

End of August he left Bursa to return by one of the coaches from Istanbul, including all his belongings, back to Germany.

N. settled in his new flat in the small town near Munich, surrounded by lush forest and, in the far distance, mountains. Most of his time, prior to his first assignment in middle September, he spent studying history, the tourist sights and the people of countries he had not only to travel to but mainly to explain to the tourists in an interesting way, abstaining from a school master's approach.

N., perhaps by intuition, worked out a way to present his clients, eager to learn more about exotic countries. He would start with a bird´s eye view of history, like sitting comfortably on a raised hunter's hide, from which one can view the past which, in turn, may explain the origin of traditions, beliefs, attitudes of the present people.

Now and then, in few intervals, he paused from his notes to reflect about his sudden changing his old profession to learning a new one.

Did he ever felt any kind of guilt? How could he jump from one to another? What was the drive, the purpose, this urge to always embrace new experiences?

Was it, as Indians would say, his Karma? Did he feel guilty of leaving behind him places and peoples he had come to love, to like?

Guilt is an attitude of the mind. The more he allowed himself to feel somewhat guilty, the greater became the cognition leading to an awareness of his self.

When he found a fly in his cup of tea, he immediately tried to rescue that poor animal. He learned that in India too. Sometimes the creature was dead. Was he guilty? Maybe it had a heart attack. Guilt? Redemption? Don't wait for Judgement Day. The secret of life is to prolong the dawn of that day, he finally concluded.

INDIA
little Tibet

Dhaulader Mountian Range

Prof.
Sondhi

Lodi Gyari

H.H. THE 14th DALAI LAMA

*Tashi Wangdi
Foreign
Minister 1984*

*The Dalia Lama
and his cat*

Across Africa and Asia

Inle Lake, Burma.

MANDARIN SINGAPORE · M

SINGAPORE · MANDARIN SINGAPORE

DAMMAM

Sheraton Dammam
HOTEL & TOWERS

YORK HOTEL

MEH KHANA BAR

HOTEL Miramar HONG KONG

Golden Temple
Amritsar, India.

On the
way to
India
1969

Sultaniye, Iran

Afganistan

SARGON HOTEL

Baghdad - Tel. {801
879

Ktesiphone
Iraq

KENJA &
TANZANIA

Kilimanjaro

Naivasha Lake

KIBO HOTEL KILIMANJARO

Ravi
Shankar

INDIA

1953

Lakshmi

The Nizam
of Hyderabad

Preparing for Himalaya shooting

Krishnamurti

Rukmini
Devi

Stephen Spender + V.S Vasan

Ladakh

Swinging to and fro Europe & India !!

Lord Ennals

Richard Gere

Geshe Ngawwang

MME. Mitterand

Petra Kelly

Dr. Van Walt

Sandhong Riponche

Demo Geneva

Oxford

M.Zoria, Press Democratic Party Republic MONGOLIA

conference Bonn 1989

Egypt 1953

Desert Police
Egypt

Mohammed
and
Hosana

Heli

Malta 2003

Hagar Qim

Valletta

Mdina

"You could imagine something cyclical in the endlessly repeated day of Brahman: before every act of creation. the old world has to be annihilated."

Hari Kunzru
"DieWandlungen des Pram Nath"
(K. Blessing Publ.. Munich)

ON THE WAY TO INDIA   1969

The tours to Great Britain and Ireland went very well. The coach driver Rudi was exceedingly well trained, helpful, polite, handling the large coach expertly through small lanes. Even the tourists, which filled the coach, were disciplined, returned from shopping sprees in time.

N. enjoyed the forty minutes talk in the morning while they were driving from one Church, Cathedral, Abbey, castle to another, entertaining them with historical stories -" 1066 and all that", bought them Irish Coffee when reaching Dun Loaghaire (from the expense account), stopping at Whisky destilleries in Scotland, and sitting with them in the homely small pubs at the country side.

Difficult, at first, were the guide books he had to use. "A famous stained glass window on the West side of this or that cathedral." Where was West? The sky was overcast, one could not find the direction. So he bought a small compass and could find out the window. Little tricks he learned by doing.

But - Great Britain and Ireland are Europe. N. was longing for the real Orient. That opportunity was given on two tours by the Persian assignment.

The coach went past Austria, Yugoslavia, Bulgaria to Edirne, Istanbul and Bogazkale, the Hittite excavation of Hattusas, through Anatolia, ancient Armenia, reaching Dogu Beyazid at the feet of Mount Ararat and the border of Iran.

On the tenth day, for N., the real Orient started.

The border guards got their backshish in form of a hundred ballpoint pens. Because of that the clearance of visa and the coach were done speedily and they entered ancient Persia.

On the way to Tabriz, N. saw a charming little mosque in the distance or was it a mausoleum?

"Can we go across there and have a stop?" he asked Rudi.

"Why not? We may have a tea there in a chaikhana."

The tiny village, Sultaniye, only had one. Some old men sat there and smoked hookas and drank tea. The owner brought out as many chairs and stools when he saw some 35 people emerging. He never had a better business. Although the conveniences were not better than those they had come across earlier, but as this trip was announced as an adventure tour, the mostly middle-aged tourists were informed. A toilet paper roll was part of their luggage.

The charming building was indeed a mausoleum. An old caretaker came along and explained in some sort of English that here was buried in 1326 Ogotai Khan, the son of Ghengiz Khan.

That gave N. the opportunity to lecture about the Mongols.

"You have learned in school that the Mongols conquered most of Asia right up to Europe. That they were brutal, cruel, massacred the population of cities. I do not see our way of warfare is much different when using nuclear bombs to destroy cities killing hundreds of thousands of people in one go, when spreading poison like Agent Orange over forests and fertile valleys, bombing cities, killing people on a massive scale.

I want to show you the other side of the Mongols, the statesmanship of rulers like Ghengiz Khan and his successors like Altan Khan who even communicated with the Vatican, they built an infrastructure throughout the empire making way to passing goods from China to Europe with post stations on the way and having a working administration in the many conquered states."

"What about religion?" someone asked.

"Originally they were Shamanists," N. replied, "but were tolerant to all other religions. They even asked Pope Innocence IV in 1242 to send priests to explain Christianity. Actually, the Buddhist king of Tibet was bestowed with the Mongol title "Dalai Lama".

At the end, having established a Mongol dynasty in China and later the Moghul dynasty in India, they became Buddhists. They brought technical know-how to Europe: the chain mail, the stirrup, the decimal system, the number zero. At the court of the Khans in Karakorum one could find civil servants from China, Armenia and Persia, medical doctors from Tibet and China, Russian aristocrats, Buddhist lamas, Zarazene sultans, ambassadors from the Khalifs in Bhagdad, Seljuk pashas from Turkey and Catholic missionaries from Rome."

The coach went on to Balbozar at the Caspian Sea. There they found a huge pool where sturgeons were happily swimming around. Sitting on the edge and holding your hand into the water, they would come and liked to be stroked.

N. bought five kilo of Caviar, Persian bread, Beer and Vodka and soon a lively party was on.

But early next morning the journey continued, Teheran and on to Isfahan.

N. was taken in of the delightfully laid out central midan the size of a football ground, surrounded by lovely mosques and palaces, created by the same architect who designed King Louis XIV's Versailles.

After that N. and his tourists got engulfed in antiquity: Persepolis, Pazargade, the palaces of Darius and Xerxes, from there to Shiraz, the birthplace of the poet Hafis (1325 - 1390). The German poet and dramatist Goethe had been influenced by Hafis nearly 450 years later.

N. did not have much time for reflections on this journey. He was on duty nearly 18 hours a day. Besides looking after the tourists during the day his responsibilities went on keeping them company in the evenings as well. Even late at night some used to knock on his hotel room and asked for postage stamps to put on the many postcards they sent home. Stamps and also money exchange belonged to his duties, as most of the elderly people did not speak any other language than their own and feared difficulties to enter strange offices.

On the other hand, N. enjoyed coach trips far more than travelling by air.

His diaries were eagerly filled. Cruising through a country gives one more to see, to take in villages ,nature, people, than flying over it. One comes to learn more of the land if one mingles with the locals, especially in small towns and resthouses on the way. Wherever N. went he found the people always friendly and eager to speak to strangers.

"If you smile at them," N. used to say, "they will smile back. This creates the first friendly contact. Smiling is a truly international language."

And what did people talk about?

"Politics is the main subject here in Teheran," an acquaintance in a hotel bar told N., "of course the Shah and his government -"

"What about Mossadeq?" N. asked.

"About him too. He is a Socialist. That, in itself, is not bad. He initiated landreform and wants to nationalize the oil exploitation - which is in American hands, and they don't like it," N. remarked.

"You are right. There are the Russian claims to import our oil. One day, Mossadeq will be silenced."

"Killed?"

"I would not put it out of question." the man said.

The people in small places, notably in villages, had different topics: the harvest, the infrastructure, their pigeons, their children, all-in-all more down to earth, more related to their often harsh lives, not interested much beyond their own small world.

"Is this not a common attitude in all small places everywhere?" N. said and they would agree over a glass of tea.

These people on the land live a simple life, uncomplicated.

Birth, weddings, funerals are their festive times.

N. was convinced that the encounter of another world, in this part of the world leads one to contemplativeness of our own hectic, confused way of life.

Next destination: Baghdad, Iraq, the cradle of a very old civilisation. N. was fascinated by the newly built Iraqi Museum. A splendid arrangement of Mesopotamian and Iraqi history from neolithic times, the developments during various epochs in antiquity, Babylon, Nebukadnezar's palaces, the Ishtar Gate, Ktesiphon, the Arab times, the building of one of the oldest universities, the Khalifs with their cultural progress, their fostering of learning, their medical schools, famous even in Europe of the Dark Ages.

The evening stroll at the Tigris. N. could imagine the Tales of One-thousand Nights, Harun al Rashid, the Khalif who in around 800 A.D. possessed a library of five-hundred books unlike many of his European counterparts who could hardly write or read.

And then on to Mossul, to ancient Ninive, Assur, through the Syrian corridor to Nusaybin in Turkey.

Back to Germany and a well earned rest of ten days. Followed by a second Iran-Tour.

The company had arranged that N. got a second passport, so that the visa could be obtained in advance from the various embassies. From there on he always had two passports.

Soon after the second Iran trip, after a short rest, finally: The Way to India. On 31 of October 1969 N. started with Mustafa in a second coach.

On the 18th day it happened on the way to Meshed. They had passed Teheran and several villages, left behind the Demavend, the holy mountain of the Persians, across the Elbruz Range, driving now on a piste across a rubble desert towards Meshed, when Rudi, the driver, looked at his watch.

"It is a little over two hours now and dusk will begin to fall."

"So we have to stop for a few minutes," N. agreed.

They stopped in the no-where amid scree, sand and lumps of rock.

"Short stop now, ladies to the left, gents to the right."

They experienced these necessary halts and laughingly got out of the coach.

Suddenly, a scream followed by loud sobs from the ladies' side. Rudi and N. hurried and found a poor lady crouching behind a boulder.

But the boulder was not what it had to be: It was a resting camel. There was a doctor on board who rushed to the scene, checking. "We have to carry her to the coach," he ordered, "she has to lie down on the rear seat. The camel has bitten her while she was squatting thinking it was a rock."

N . looked around and found a number of resting camels, blending into the scenery in the dusk. Rudi ran to his tool compartment and took out an air-filled tube from one spare tyre, emptied the rear seat in the coach from someone's belongings. The lady was carefully laid down. The doctor did some first aid while the rest waited outside.

"She has to be taken to hospital for stitching. Where is the next stop?"

"About an hour in Meshed. They ought to have a hospital there."

The coach reached Meshed in about an hour's drive. They found a hospital, the lady was well treated but had to stay overnight there to be on the safe side. The coach would collect her next morning.

"There is always the unexpected", Rudi muttered when they reached their hotel.

"That is, in a way, what makes an adventure so interesting," N. said.

Meshed is one of the holy places for Muslims. But for N. it was very important, because it was the birthplace of Omar Khayyam (1050 - 1120), this unorthodox Sufi whose seemingly erotic verses and his often mentioned wine drinking contain a symbolism to be understood on a higher level, a transcendence, a mystical dedication of the kind which Catholic nuns use when they refer to themselves as "Brides of Jesu".

This referring to wine drinking is nothing else but to take in Divine Wisdom, the Nectar of the Greeks, the Soma of Hindus.

Omar Khayyam has discovered a reality which corresponds to the reality concept of Buddhism as well as that of existential philosophy of Sartre and Bertrand Russell.

"Oft before I swore repentance every day, but was I sober when I swore?

And then came spring, and roses and wine.

My threadbare repentance was torn up at once."

> "Oh, make the most of what we yet may spend
> before we too into the dust descend.
> Dust into dust, and under dust to lie
> no Wine, no Song, no Singer
> and - no end."

Nirvana, the Emptiness, or, as the Existentialists would say: The absolute Existence, explains Omar thus:

"This old caravanserai called the world, sometimes nightly dark, soon alight at day, is nothing but a leftover from past glories, where kings, praiseworthy in their time, lie buried in eternity. They rest in dust who once rotated around the centre of the world. Alive, they used to lay in dust of their own arrogance, their word was nothing but empty sound, now gone with the wind."

The two coaches reached Afghanistan on the 19th day.

The lady in N's coach had recovered quickly from her treatment at the hospital and was cheerfully resting on the back bench of the coach.

Along the Paranomisus Range and passing hundreds of windmills, they entered Herat in the late afternoon.

Operating from June to September only - the time of the wheat harvest - N., at first, could not make out that they were windmills, because they were lacking the huge wheeled arms as in Europe. The lower part consists of a square mud-walled room housing the millstones. The mill shaft is made from white poplar and rises through the arched roof of the mill house. To this shaft are attached six sails to each of which reed mats are affixed. These sails spin between walls on two sides forming a well which aids in funnelling the wind.

These mills were used already in ancient Khorasan, the old name of this part of Afghanistan.

Herat was famous for its covered bazaars. Light filtered down from windows below the barrel vaulting of the ceiling onto the shops. In ancient times these shops were filled with damascened swords, bows inlaid with jade and tourmaline from Mongol - China, drinking cups of Arabian coral, illuminated books and silk from Herat, Bukhara rugs, unbored pearls and golden images from India. Fruit stalls offered such delicacies as rhubarb from Kabul, bananas from Isfahan and juicy oranges from far off Damascus.

Herat was a busy junction of caravan routes from various parts of Asia. During the centuries the covered bazaars dilapidated, were finally torn down.

Today some have been restored among the tree-lined streets in the city and the tourists enjoyed their evening stroll.

Along the banks of the Hari Rud river the roads were not more than a track which oriented itself by following telegraph poles. Through the Dashti Margo, the Desert of Death, they travelled via Girisk to Kandahar, founded in 320 B.C. by Alexander the Great.

Everywhere wonderful mosques, mausoleums, delightful covered with Lapislazuli inlaid tiles. Gazni, the old capital of tribal kings with its castle, old city walls, tall minarets - the way to Kabul.

Kabul itself was disappointing for N., dirty, partly destroyed by numerous tribal wars. The smelly Kabul River was used by inhabitants as public conveniences as well by women doing their washing. Different appeared the new city with its government buildings, the king's residence and the bazaar.

"Here we have to do some buying of Pakistani and Indian rupees," Mustafa said, who always seemed to have inside information, "even for the return trip later. It is cheaper here."

While the tourists were looked after by local guides, Mustafa and N. went to the bazaar, haggled over exchange rates and got rather huge amounts of Rupees, which, in turn, they would use during the coming weeks to pay for petrol, servicing the coaches and to change money for the tourists against the official bank rates in Pakistan and India.

The highlight was the excursion through narrow serpentine roads in hired taxis along the majestic Hindukush mountain range to Bhamian, 3400 m above sea level, to admire the tall Buddhist statues carved out of the rocks.

Then Jallalabad which had seen many battles between British troops from British India and later the Russians. Both never could set foot in Afghanistan and were always thrown out.

Afghanistan, N. summed up, has a delightful charm of its own. Although mainly barren, the underground irrigation system, the Khanat, invented some 2000 years ago by the Persians, supplied fresh water to fields, villages and towns. Khanats are wells, vertically dug to ground water level, connected by tunnels, also dug out to ground water level.

These tunnels are several kilometres long and the water is clear and cold. The climate is hot in summer, freezing cold in winter. Majestic mountain ranges in the north, extraordinary architecture of mosques, fortified castles, impressive old town gates, above all: clear air to breathe - it was for N. and his group of travellers like entering a different and interesting world with kind and hospitable peoples.

Political, Afghanistan was never quite united in its long history, it was always prey to invaders on their way to India.

Through the Tangi Guru Gorge and the famous Khyber Pass they finally, on the 26th day, reached Pakistan.

They stayed overnight in a rest house near the ruins of an old settlement, Taxila, founded in the 7th century B.C.

The old name Tak Hasila is mentioned in the Hindu epos Mahabharata as well as in Buddhist texts. In Persepolis on the mausoleum of Darius the name given was Taxile and was a provincial capital of Persia. After the conversion to Buddhism of Emperor Ashoka, around 500 B.C. it became a Buddhist city with an university, monasteries, stupas, a seat of high learning. It was from here that Emperor Ashoka sent buddhist monks to Alexandria in Egypt, where they made contact with the Essenes, but that is another story.

At the time of Alexander the Great, around 320 B.C., Taxila was the capital city of an Indian kingdom. The Mongols destroyed it in 455 A.D. The ruins were discovered only in 1912.

After their evening meal, sitting outside the rest house around an open fire, they all took in the magic of the night. One of the travellers, Rox Schulz, a famous documentary film maker, took out his Guitar and strummed a few notes, forming a soft melody which enhanced the mood.

The full moon did his best to take his part, while N. reflected, and felt to say an ancient Indian prayer, the Gayatri. The air was velvety and somehow electrified. The flames seemed to make the nature, the bushes, the trees alive. The travellers sat, sipped some wine and just quietly let their thoughts wonder around until the thoughts were gone and the great emptiness created a mind full of peace and happiness.

When, finally, all of them went into their rooms to sleep, N. sat for an hour or so by himself. This was one of the rare moments during the journey when he could sit and think, undisturbed.

The full moon and millions of stars looked down. From far away a dog barked, answered by another. Otherwise the peace, the stillness were overwhelming.

"What I am doing here?" N. asked himself. This journey is full of past places, of past people who invented irrigation, barrel vaults, who had lived between birth, weddings and funerals, of kings, rulers whose deeds we want to know. Do we compare all this past with our way of life, which we declare to be superior?

"History is the lie about which one has reached agreement." Napoleon once said. That is the political, pragmatic explanation. But there also is a law of historical credit: He who is wrong had to pay. He who was right would have been absolved. But what is right, what is wrong? In the end one has to confess that virtue does not matter in history.

And what about the history of the individual human being? Is man, as Emerson concluded, explicable by nothing less than all his own history?

"If the whole of history is one person, it is all explained from individual experience. There is a relation between the hours of our life and the centuries of time."

And N's experience? In it lays an explanation not only of his history but also of the experience of other living people.

The origin of life, N. followed this up, of all living beings form a chain.

"Every time you fell a tree, a star falls from heaven," this word of Krishnamurti came to N's mind. What may happen on the day when people have felled all trees?

Do human beings ever have learned from history? Have they ever really learned from their own experience?

Finally, N. put out the smouldering wood-ashes and left the atmospheric place to go to bed.

Next morning, a number of travellers thanked Mustafa and N. for this unforgettable night.

But the caravan had to move on.

Peshawar was left behind and Lahore, the provincial capital of Punjab, was the next place. It was there, some years ago, where Ava Gardner and Cary Grant were filming "Bhowane Junction" and stayed at the same hotel, the Maidens, a nice old-fashioned, colonial building of the days of the Raj.

Lahore once belonged to Afghan rulers, then to the Moghul Emperor Akbar the Great who built the fortified castle and the mighty city walls, Shah Jehan the ornamented palace, Aurangzep the mosque. The Afghans took over for a while, in 1761 the Sikhs occupied it and, in 1849 the British ruled up to 1947.

On the 29th day they reached the Indian border. A short drive brought them to Amritsar, the holy city of the Sikhs with its magnificent Golden Temple. N. felt almost at home, driving on passable roads with uninterrupted traffic. Cars, cycles, carts, camels, horses, buffaloes and people, heat and dust and a babble of voices. From Delhi on to Agra, a must for all tourists.

Although admiring the architectural balance of this famous mausoleum and the intricate workmanship of the filigran marble, N. found it a little too much of elaborate sweetness.

Benares was teeming with people, thousands of Hindu pilgrims coming every day, taking their ritual bath in the dirty Ganges. But what a difference to Sarnath, a short drive away, with its quiet deer park, where Gautama is said to have reached Buddhahood, having discovered the Middle Way - no opposite, no ascetic, no indulgent life - to enlightenment.

Down southwards through central India, passing through avenues of bodhi-trees to Haiderabad, which N. knew from previous visits, to the garden city Bangalore to Madras. There they visited the crypt of the Cathedral in which the apostle Thomas was buried in approximately 50 A.D. The crypt is the oldest part of the newer St. Thomas Cathedral.

Innumerable temples in the distinct south Indian style, along paddocks, to Madurai with an assembly of hundreds of Hindu temples their slanting towers richly decorated with sculptures.

And then the southern-most part: Cape Cormorin. No temples, no hectic, just a day of rest, swimming and bathing in the clear Indian Ocean.

Passing along the western coast through Kerala, on the left the Indian Ocean, on the right villages and small towns amidst temples, very neatly white-washed churches with slender steeples looking rather continental European. These belong to the St. Thomas community. From here the apostle started his mission in India some years after Jesu death.

Via Poona, a drive through imposing scenery, the most interesting Buddhist cave temple at Karli, dating back to the 1st century B.C., then the steep gorges of Bore Ghat finally to Bombay.

The 50th day was spent seeing the sights of this busy city, bustling with millions of inhabitants. They stayed at the Juhu Beach Hotel, while the tourists were packing, Mustafa and N. had a short, well-earned rest until the farewell party on the beach with much laughter, music, drinks and talk of their adventurous journey.

The 51st day, using the coaches for the last time, saw their departure by air back to Germany.

The two coaches were brought to the Mercedes agency for overhaul servicing, while Mustafa and N. finished the accounts for Holter's company, counted their own profits from money changing and a huge amount of tips and then had four days rest.

The next group would come on Christmas eve, and the same tour would start through India and find its way back overland back to Germany.

One member of the new group brought a small parcel for N, containing money to be used for the return journey.

After another 51 days N. had two weeks rest in his small flat near Munich, before his new assignment: East Africa in 1970.

"Funny," N. mused, "I always see old places again for different reasons, though."

DIVERTISSEMENT

Being on a short visit to Germany, I was able to meet with N. shortly before he had to leave for East Africa.

"How do you feel?" I asked.

"Quite well, it is a hard job as far as my back is concerned, sitting most of the day in a coach, but very interesting though. You learn more of the countries driving through them." N. replied.

I had gone through his diaries which he had kept with me, having read through them up to 1960. Apart from N's personal reflections which he had jotted down in detail, there were a number of questions though to discuss about the dialogues between him and the people he had met.

These dialogues were not given in his diaries in full, there were only short notices whom he had met and some remarks what was said. So I had to re-construct these parts.

He agreed.

Another big question was why he did not mention his love life apart from meeting Heli in Egypt, and, to a rather unsuccessful short meeting with Lakshmi in India.

"I have not told everything in my diaries," he replied, "why should I? To make the book more popular, more saleable? I know a number of books where the author does not even mention making love."

"These are very few," I interrupted.

"May be, but they are quite good and, obviously, they don't cater for popular demand. That annoys me in many films also. People expect lurid sequences of sex scenes together with hideous action scenes such as cars flying through the air and much killing. If they don't make love, they shoot each other. I detest these stories. Anyway everybody has something in a secret chamber within himself. During the years you simply forget where and when you have lost the key to unlock the chamber."

"There is no way to unlock your chamber?" I asked.

"No," N. answered. "because whatever you do, yesterday or today ends in the past and only chance changes it into faintly remembering."

"That sounds like Krishnamurti."

"I admit, he has changed my way of thinking, but much more my understanding of life a great deal, but so have, to a smaller extend, others like Russell and Montaigne. My way of looking at things is composed from many sources.

"That also means, that you are not free.." I suggested.

"No, I am not totally free, still a prisoner," N. answered, "but I try to free myself, at least I am on the way. To be free does not mean death, but perhaps, wisdom. The same goes for faith, religious or otherwise."

"There are many people who will not agree," I remarked.

"Of course, they would not," N. replied, "Faith is only, if at all, a very small part of truth. There never is an absolute truth. It would be unthinkable, even dangerous, if a human being would know The Truth.

I refilled our glasses and could not resist to mention Omar Khayyam:

"There is a small part of truth in this glass of wine."

"Of course, there is," N. laughed, "you know what? One should invest money in wine. Where else do you get twelve per cent?"

"Yes," I agreed, "money does grow on trees, only the bank owns all the branches."

On this note our evening closed in a merry wine mood.

KENYA AND TANZANIA 1970

N. had to fly to Mombasa to await the empty coach arriving by sea. He stayed at the Manor Hotel for a few days until the shipping agency would inform him of the arrival. So he had a few days at leisure, studying road maps, hotels and lodges on the way. Holter's company had done a splendid job arranging things in advance.

He would have to collect the first group at Nairobi's airport and take them to their accommodation at the Westwood Park Country Club in the fashionable suburb of Karen. This part of Nairobi had been named in honour of Karen Blixen, the famous Danish author who had, in the early 1900's, fallen in love with Kenya, then a British colony. As a matter of fact the main building on the estate, now containing the reception, kitchen, dining room, a very cosy well stocked bar, surrounded by a large veranda in front of a well kept lawn, was the house where Karen Blixen used to live. Added were several bungalows and a swimming pool.

From this place, the 26 days' tour would start, provided the coach would arrive in Mombasa in time.

It did arrive only with one day delay. It took a huge crane some hours to heave the large vehicle off the small freighter. Once safely on the quay, Rudi, who had accompanied the coach, got busy attaching the batteries, filling the tanks, checking various technical details, filling in custom forms and off they went on a reasonable tarmac road.

It was late afternoon on 20th February, 1970.

"Rudi, you have to take care, when you see signs "Animal have Right of Way", N. cautioned, "elephants love to rub themselves preferably on big lorries and buses."

"I am prepared," Rudi nodded, also looking forward to his first-time visit to Africa south of the Sahara.

Shortly before they reached Mtito Andei, their over night stop about half way towards Nairobi, they halted looking at a lorry, the bonnet being severely damaged, smashed in by the weight of an elephant trotting away with a group of his family. The lorry driver and others argued, because the driver had paid no attention to the sign.

"See what I mean?" N. said.

The lodge was a most up-to-date building, it had a refreshing swimming pool, an inviting bar, good food and friendly service.

"Welcome, Bwana."

They sat and enjoyed Rudi's first night. Rudi handed over instructions and money from the company. The doors to their rooms were difficult to close, they were screeching. The reason was a number of big, black beetles which got stuck on the threshold. When they brushed the dead bodies away the doors could be closed.

Another experience of Africa's wildlife.

The Westwood Park proved to be an excellent "Headquarter", there was ample parking space. N. immediately made friends with Jacques the quirly French manager, Mr. Tolley, a retired British permanent resident, with Odinga, the night watchman and his Alsatian dog Sammy.

Sammy, although a very friendly dog, had an aversion against certain coloured people. And it happened on Sunday, when Nairobi's top people from the business community and members of the diplomatic corps came for the famous buffet lunch, when Sammy disliked the leg of an African diplomat. The dog gnarled and took a bite. The diplomat, not acting diplomatically, called the police and ordered them to shoot the dog. Jacques, with N's help, quickly got Sammy out of the way and it found refuge in N's bungalow. The police searched the large compound but did not find the dog. "It must have run away", Jacques explained to the officer. N. kept Sammy the rest of the day and the whole night, he gave it food and Sammy slept peacefully on the rug in front of N's bed.

Next morning, the air being clean, Sammy returned and resumed its duty, and everybody was happy.

The tourists arrived from Munich by Egypt Air at two in the morning.

N. welcomed them at the airport, passed them through passport control and customs. The coach brought them to Westwood Park where they went to sleep after the long flight.

N. was very pleased to see among the tourists Karel de Munter from Holland. They had met years ago on board the ship which brought them from Australia to Greece, and had become good friends.

Early afternoon, next day, they started the tour of Nairobi city and the Nairobi National Park, they saw their first lions, cameras were clicking, and proceeded to the Animal Orphanage on Langata Road. Here, sponsored by the World Wildlife Fund, sick and abandoned wild animals are cared for until they can be released to fend for themselves.

On the 5th day, early morning, they drove to Naivasha Lake. During the drive he told the passenger to drink much water and to use a fair amount of salt with the meals, the climate under the equator demands this. All, but one lady objected, because she was on a saltless diet.

Naivasha Lake in the morning mist was an unforgettable sight: Nearly a million flamingoes congregate there, making this lake one of the most fascinating and rewarding bird sanctuaries in the world. When the mist slowly disappears the birds would rise forming a huge pink cloud to settle down again to continue their morning meal and, as N. pointed out, telling each other the dreams they had the night before.

After lunch, they drove on a secondary road to see the majestic Nyahururu Falls, pausing for a photo stop at the equator sign, back via Nakuru to Nairobi, where the evening meal was waiting. The tourists were happily reloading films into their cameras for the coming day.

The next day started on a dusty piste along the Ngong Hills and Magadi to the Masai Mara Game Reserve, a good spot to see a great number of plains game antelopes, gazelles in big numbers.

Here they encountered their first Masai, the men very proud looking, the women adorned with huge necklaces made of colourful glass pearls. Back to Nairobi for lunch and off to the famous Serengeti. They stayed at a comfortable lodge in Namanga, right at the border to Tanzania.

There was time to mingle with the many Masai. They showed us their manyattas, small mud huts, the compound surrounded by a thick wall of thornbushes to keep wild animals away from their cattle and goats inside. N. explained that, if a young Masai is interested in a particular girl, he would go to see her, ram his spear in front of her doorway - usually a large piece of animal skin - and nobody would dare to disturb them.

The Masai do not kill their cattle, they are their most precious possession and the wealth of a clan is seen by the number of beasts they own. Their staple food consists of maize, milk and blood. They would shoot a small arrow into the vein at the neck of a cow, extract a certain quantity of blood and close the wound with a mixture of herbs and mud. Milk and blood are mixed together in calabasses. This, in turn, is mixed with maize. That type of nourishment contains all the vitamins and minerals one needs.

The next morning they were on the way to Arusha.

Politically, President Nyerere had it easier than Obote in Uganda. There were not so many different tribes in Tanzania who would fight each other. Nyerere, a teacher by profession, had developed the idea of Jami'a which means, in Arabic, a family clan living in common unity with common traditions, aspirations and a common way of life. This thought he enlarged to the family of tribes forming one nation.

The Arusha Hotel is a comfortable place featuring a remarkable bar with an even more remarkable barkeeper who entertained his guests with interesting stories about the recent filming of "Hatari". John Wayne together with Hardy Krüger filmed in Serengeti and in and around Arusha. John Wayne, the hero of many Western, was afraid to be confronted with wild animals, some scenes had to be taken by a double, whereas Hardy Krüger, a reckless and daring German actor, was the opposite. Many photos displayed in the bar told their own stories of the shooting.

On the 27th February the group arrived at the Ngorongoro Crater Lodge and, from there, admired an impressive view over the Olduvai Gorge, where, some years ago, Professor Leakey discovered one of the oldest human remains, and the vast plains of the Serengeti, now and then dotted with umbrella-like Acacia trees.

The following day, using the coach carefully down on serpentines they, accompanied by a game warden, proceeded to a spot down on the ground when the warden told Rudi to stop here and advised the tourists not to leave the immediate vicinity of the coach. In the distance clouds of dust were seen and the grumble of a million hoofs could be heard. The tourists thought of an approaching thunderstorm,but it was not the case. After a few minutes the dust clouds and the grumble came nearer and they suddenly watched with awe the passing-by of innumerable animals: This was a sight only to be seen twice a year - the galloping of wild animals to greener pastures at the western half of the Serengeti plains.

Zebras, buffalos, wildebeest, herds of antelopes, gazelles of all sizes, followed by slower beasts like elephants and graceful giraffes passed by the thousands.

Karel de Munter managed to climb on the roof of the coach to film this spectacle.

This adventure was by far the highlight of the day if not of the whole tour. Cameras could not be clicked fast enough, the tourists were delighted and thanked the game warden to have the coach stopped in time, it would have been smashed by the sheer force of millions of animals. That night at the Crater Hotel the talk finished late.

Early next morning,stopping shortly at Manyara to watch lions resting on thick branches to digest their meal from last night's prowl.

In the afternoon, via Arusha on a pott-holed gravel road they reached Momella Lodge, owned by Hardy Krüger, Round the main house there were stone-built round huts with thatched roofs like native roundables, but installed with twin beds and showers. Mount Kilimanjaro was clouded, as usual, but during sunset the clouds lifted for a few minutes.

The people came out of the showers, scantily dressed, cameras in hand, to watch this rare sight of a snowcapped mountain right under the equator. For N. and the others this too was an experience not likely to be seen again.

Except for the fact, that at night one of the thatched roofs was eaten up by a hungry giraffe.

Via Moshi and Voi, the following day they reached Mombasa for a well earned rest on the beach for two days, swimming, lazing about or going for a short trip to the souvenir shops in town.

On the long drive from Mombasa to Nairobi the lady who did not take salt collapsed and had to be brought to the Nairobi Hospital for treatment.

The last day was busy with packing. N. went to the hospital to collect the lady. When N. asked the doctor what he had done to make her fit so soon he answered, in the presence of the lady: "I gave her a strong salt injection, that was all she needed."

The farewell party took much of the night. The plane left at three in the morning.

For N. and Rudi there were two free days during which the coach had to be serviced. N. tried to cure his back ache to be fit for the next group to arrive.

On the final day of the next group, Rudi fell ill with fever. Diagnosis at the hospital: Malaria. N. immediately cabled Holter to send a replacement for Rudi.

Then N. went to see how Rudi was going on.

"You will not believe it," Rudi said, "I don't know how they treated me, but when I woke up I thought I was dreaming. There was a jetblack nurse smiling at me and said in perfect German how I feel and whether I was hungry."

"It so happened that this particular nurse had been trained in Germany, and I thought it would be nice to have her look after Rudi," the doctor explained, "and, by the way, we used a newly developed treatment, which will result, that Rudi never again will suffer from malaria."

That was good news indeed. Rudi was still a bit weak but agreed to be sent back with the next group.

The new driver, Sepp, arrived with the new group and N. could show him the route. Sepp also was a polite and experienced driver, did many other tours with Holters and "knew the ropes". N. had to make a number of trips, enduring the pain in his back. One day, while in Nairobi, two smartly dressed gentlemen asked N. for an interview.

N. was relieved that these men were not secret agents of some sort, but they wanted to make an offer. They had watched him in Nairobi organising the tours, looking after the tourists, and were generally impressed by the way he handled everything. They offered him to work for the newly founded agency belonging to one of the biggest German department stores with chains in nearly every town. The new job would contain the managing of logistic, that means to collect incoming tourists at the airport, distribute them into small mini buses which would take them to their previously booked Safari Lodges where they were guided by local guides. Only those who had booked for the Westwood Park Country Club he had to look after, selling them safaris within the vicinity of Nairobi. He did not have to accompany them. He would have a rented car at his disposal. That sounded too good to be true: The salary would be the same, he could retain his headquarters in the Club and did not have to sit for weeks on buses, thus helping his aching back to be relieved.

He gave notice to Holters on health reasons and asked for relief. The last journey for N. started with Mrs. Stanzel to be introduced to the tour. She also was a very experienced tour guide, having done several tours for Holters in Ethiopia. She was very helpful and with her charming female approach won the hearts of the guests at once.

N's contract was terminated on 15th May 1971. On the 16th he went with the general manager of the new company to the airport meeting Mr. Blok, the owner of two large renowned hotels in Nairobi, and Hardy Krüger, the German actor and owner of Momella Lodge, as their pilot. They boarded the small Cherokee plane and Hardy showed off his skill as a daring pilot, curving around the sky to Mombasa.

There at the Beach Hotel N's contract was duly signed, as well as contracts with the hotel owners.

It was followed by a hilarious party at the swimming pool with a good dinner and plenty of drinks during which Hardy fell into the pool amidst the applause of the others.

N. preferred to go back by train to Nairobi. Much as he liked Hardy Krüger, he would not risk a reckless return flight on the small plane.

At the station he bought a newspaper and learned that the army in Uganda had made a coup d´etat under Amin and that he was installed as president, while Oboto could escape to Tanzania.

The groups for the new company arrived once a week, usually at one o'clock in the morning. N. drove in his car to and from the airport after having seen to it that all guests were driven by minibuses to their booked safari lodges. The mini buses he had arranged with Thorntree Safari, an old and reliable company for hiring buses in Nairobi.

In the morning after arrival, N. would welcome the tourists, explain how things worked in Kenya and sold them local day tours in his old friendly and charming way, telling jokes, giving advice and having a wonderful time.

"My name is Matter," a well dressed tourist came up to N. at the hotel reception," I want to shoot a lion or cheetah, can you help me?"

"Of course, Mr. Matter, I shall find out the availability, because you will have to be accompanied by a professional hunter who also is a game warden. Shall we say ,this afternoon at the bar?"

That gave N. time to make some phone calls to the director of Thorntree Safari, who after a few hours send a messenger with papers to be signed, people to be hired, transport to be arranged, a white hunter to be employed, and weapons to be given by the authorities.

In the afternoon, Mr. and Mrs. Matter waited eagerly for N. in the bar who could explain everything.

"Your group will consists of two jeeps, one for you and the hunter because he is the only one who knows where and when the animals are to be found. The second jeep is manned by the cook, with helpers, with tents, folding chairs, table, crockery, food and water. Alcoholic drinks you will have to supply yourself. You will be allowed to shoot one single animal only after you have followed it for a day or two with the help of the white hunter. And, of course, you will be handed a gun and ammunition. The price for all this is quite high -"

"Look, N." Matter interrupted, "I can afford all this. I shall pay all the fees in advance."

The deal was settled and Mr. and Mrs. Matter went, after waiting two days for the permits, happily on their own safari.

One day later - N. had made some inquiries at the German embassy where he learned that the gentleman in question is a millionaire and owner of several well known restaurants.

After nearly five days they were back.

"Well, Mr. Matter, did you get your animal?"

"No." he replied, "we had to follow a beautiful leopard for about two days, when I saw that graceful animal I simply could not shoot. I went back, having had a wonderful experience."

From that day on Mr. Matter became N's friend.

Groups came and went. Some people did not want to hear N's advice not to drink ice cold beer and then go for a swim in the unshaded swimming pool, and collapsed with severe stomach trouble. But most enjoyed a lovely time they had, eagerly expressing their delight at what they had seen.

So, time went on, until the blow came in April 1972. All contracts with foreigners had to be terminated if a particular job could have been done by a Kenyan.

He left Kenya. Back in Germany he had time to think and developed the idea of opening his own office as tourist consultant, working out very individualistic tours for very small groups of two or four. He would arrange with airlines, hotels and transport companies for cars or mini busses and accompany the people as guide. Of course, they would have to pay for this type of de luxe tours. But by now he knew how to negotiate with airlines, hotels and transport companies. It was a special niche which other agencies, with perhaps the exception of Thomas Cooks, had not thought of.

But first he contacted an embassy in Bonn where he met another "uncle".

After a few days they received an o.k. from their far away headquarters, resulting in an assignment to go to Pakistan by the end of May.

"Back to the old game," smiled N. and left, after obtaining the necessary visa, Germany via Moscow to Karachi.

PAKISTAN 1972 and 1974

N. stays for a couple of days at the Metropole Hotel. His old friends were all gone. Dr. Z. and his family had left for Germany, the German Reading Room had been closed down, his diplomatic friends would have gone too.

He boards the train to Rawalpindi, his point of directive. On that long trip he reflects on his assignment. Pakistan has changed, even the street names in Karachi have been altered.

Politically, the attitude towards India had changed. That is the reason why he was not allowed to fly via Delhi to Karachi but to use the route via Moscow. The president, Ali Khan Butto, a member of the twenty-three richest families, has not achieved a sound economy and has to rely on Islamic states and western industrialized countries for support. The military clash with India over Kashmir is not settled at all. Karachi, N. felt, is not the old easy going city he knew. The people look listless.

His objective is twofold. Firstly he has to deliver a sealed envelope to Wali Khan, living somewhere near Rawalpindi and Peshawar. He had to find out. Wali Khan is some sort of Eminence grise, a shrewd politician, a revered personality among his ethnic group, the Pathans who live on both sides of the Pakistan-Afghanistan border, a man with useful contacts. Civil unrest had developed in Afghanistan due to the weakness of the king, and the provincial governors are on the way to become warlords. In this situation Wali Khan uses his tremendous influence from the safe haven of Pakistan.

Secondly, N. has to report on the general outlook, the mood of the people, economic and military information if possible.

While the train, slow like in India, rumbles along, the click-clack on the rails makes him sleepy.

Next day, in Rawalpindi, he puts up at a small and simple place proudly called Lord's Hotel, situated in Adamjee Road near the bazaar.

From the manager N. inquired to find a reliable taxi driver for a full day who could find the whereabouts of Wali Khan. The manager, at first, looks astonished, but then smiles. Already next morning, a taxi driver comes to the hotel and promises to take N. to Wali Khan and back the same day. They haggle over the price and leave right away.

Leaving the tarmac road outside Rawalpindi, the car jogs along through sandy side paths, through hamlets with mud huts among apricot trees, fields, grazing sheep, stopping now and then in tiny villages to ask for direction. Awe inspiring mountain ranges loom in the distance.

After some hours they reach, in the middle of nowhere, a large compound surrounded by a high mesh wire fence beyond which, nearly hidden by trees and shrubs, a grand looking stone house with a properly tiled roof is seen. At the gate a guard stops them and after some discussion and a phone call to someone in the house the gate is opened and the taxi moves towards the mansion. Some other guard leads N. into the house, leaving the taxi waiting outside.

"Please, come in and wait here," the guard opened the door to a spacious room comfortably furnished with easy chairs and Kashmiri side tables.

Two white gentlemen inside look at N. with curiosity.

"Waiting here long?" N. asks.

"Nearly two hours. The old man seems to be very busy." the older of the two replies. They exchange cards. N. looks at the older one.

"I did not know that the USA has a representative in Peshawar?"

"Well, we have to be everywhere," Mr. Pingitore, the director of the American Center answers.

"I think we know each other," the younger man says looking at N. who had not given a visiting card, "my name is John Kierman."

"Kierman - well, of course, that was some 14 years ago in Karachi.

You must be the son. I remember "Cocktails and Carols at the Kiermans."

N. smiles, "you were a teenager then."

"That's right."

"And now you work for the same firm?"

"You may call it that way." Kierman jr. answered.

"It is a small world," N. muses, "and so we meet in an obscure house somewhere on the western border on -"

"- on business," Mr. Pingitore interrupts."

"Of course, so am I."

The door opens and a Pakistani appears.

"I am the secretary of Wali Khan Sahib.. He wants to see Mr. N. first, if you don't mind," this to the two waiting men, "it will not take long."

He leads N. through a small corridor into another room where he finds an impressive looking, white bearded man sitting behind a desk, getting up and stretching out his hand.

"I understand you have something for me?" he asks..

"Yes, Sir." N. reaches inside his pocket and takes out the sealed envelope and puts it across the desk into the hand of Wali Khan, "Is there anything you want me to convey to my client?"

Wali Khan inspects the seal and puts the envelope into a drawer of his desk.

"No, nothing. We shall be in contact with your client. Thank you very much for coming here to deliver this letter. May God be with you."

The secretary leads N. out of the room, back into the waiting room.

"Would you like some tea?" he offers and leads the two Americans to Wali Khan. N. sits down when a servant comes and brings him tea. Then he opens the door and waves to the guard standing outside.

"I am leaving now."

The guard takes him to the front door, where his taxi waits and off they go returning to Rawalpindi.

Meeting the CIA people at Wali Khan's house has to be entered into the report, N. thinks. His "client" will love that.

In Rawalpindi N. decides to go back to Karachi. The train leaves the same night. N. settles the hotel bill, gets to the station, paying his sleeper 1st class ticket, has a quick meal at the station restaurant, boards the train and is off for Karachi relieved to have passed on this sealed letter.

Back in Karachi he meets, more or less by accident, a number of people during the following days at the bar of the Metropole Hotel.

Among them Mr. Khatib, General Secretary of the Federation of Trade Union, who gives N. a gloomy view of the labour situation of Pakistan's present economic low. He meets Akbar Ali who is looking for a German business contact for obtaining certain goods for the Ministry of Defence, including a patrol boat. And, a few hours before departure, he meets Abbas Lakdawala, a manufacturer of plastic household goods, but also having contracts with the army.

N. puts all this information into his final report and leaves for the airport.

Back in Bonn, "uncle" was more than pleased.

They worked out a cover for N. In his new job as tourist consultant: he is supposed to be keen on developing tourism in the northwest frontier area of Pakistan. Murree is already known as a popular summer resort, situated in an altitude of nearly eight-thousand feet above sea level having some good hotels amidst a fir-scented landscape with giant pine trees. From there one could develop Swat valley, nearly fourteen-thousand feet high, towered by snow-capped mountains, flower-covered slopes and fruit laden orchards, and, of course, Gilgit, bordering on Afghanistan and, to the north, on China, but at present still a sensitive area out of bounds for normal travellers.

N. had to do much correspondence with Akbar Ali and Lakdawala, to get them interested. And, indeed, they were.

N. was told to concentrate on Lakdawala's business in Karachi and to find out more of Akbar Ali's import plans. The correspondence revealed that Akbar Ali was interested in obtaining electronic devices, such as "infrared line scan cameras to be fitted in pods at a speed of 15,000 km/hr for Mirage aircraft, gun sights for tanks, infrared screens for submarine telescopes for the Naval Intelligence Directorate in Islamabad."

This was, of course, far beyond N's capacity, but "uncle" was impressed by the equipment, Pakistan wanted to obtain. And that by open letters.

A sure sign of preparation for another military clash against India? It took almost two years to work all this out. Finally, in March 1974, N. started his second assignment He again boarded the plane via Moscow to Karachi, but this time he could stay at the new Intercontinental Hotel in Karachi, because his allowance would permit it.

Lakdawala and N. meet at the Gymkhana Club for what is known to be a business lunch.

The Pakistani entrepreneur has already worked out plans to develop tourism in Swat Valley, including costs of buildings of bungalow-type hotels, costs of personnel needed for running the hotels.

"There are two difficulties", Lakdawala explains, "the Gilgit Valley is still forbidden territory, the army would not think of changing that. The second are bathroom facilities and stainless steel kitchen equipment. The government is very stringent on issuing import permits, and these would have to be imported. You understand that the economic situation is by far not solved."

"And what about your army connection?" N. asks.

"For the army, of course, import permits are issued, so for instance for the necessary raw materials I need, but not for kitchen sinks and toilets. I get these other things from Germany."

"And what are the 'other things' you get imported?"

"Mainly granulates for household goods, but of a stronger kind."

"But may it not be easier to get them from Great Britain, due to the Commonwealth connection?" N. wants to know.

"In 1972, soon after you left, Pakistan left the Commonwealth. After the heavy involvement of the army to quell the uprising in East Pakistan and the following declaration of Independence of East Pakistan, now called Bangladesh, things have changed drastically. President Bhutto was re-elected but he is losing out on the support from the army."

Lakdawala invites N. to come next day to see his factory, as N. will stay only for a few days.

And that is why N. had come here in the first place. The touristic development, actually, was put up for show.

In most large cities in the world the industrial areas seldom can be called beautiful. Karachi is no exception. There are small ramshackle, broken down sheds almost falling to pieces, busy tradesmen producing whatever it is, some repair shops, people hammering in smoked-stained open huts but, in between, some larger well kept factories.

The taxi stops at a compound, enclosed by a fence with a nicely wrought-iron sign: "Golden Industries" above the entrance. A neat large building, housing the office and workshops - that is Lakdawala's realm at Sharah-e-Liaquat, Karachi 2.

He stands at the door and greets N.

"Welcome, let us go in."

Inside, a well equipped office with a large desk covered by papers, catalogues, comfortable easy chairs and highly polished wooden side tables.

He rings a bell, and a servant appears.

"Chai," he calls out and, within minutes steaming tea is served.

"Golden Industries is a well chosen name," N. mentions.

"It is on this compound where I started off years ago in a shed with a corrugated iron roof and a small amount of machinery making the casing for fountain pens," Lakdawala proudly smiles, "after years passed by and fountain pens, after the invention of ballpoint pens, went out of demand, I could build this house and enlarge production of other things."

"Impressive," N. remarks.

"My main products are household goods like buckets, plates, small tubs - everything plastic.

"And then the army came in".

"Yes, you will laugh at this: Their first order was for uniform buttons in a hard durable plastic."

"Plastic buttons the soldiers don't have to polish as they had to with brass ones," N. interrupts.

"Quite so, but hard plastic demands another type of raw material,"

116

Lakdawala explains, "you see, for Buckets and this sort of thing, you need polystyrol which is, like all the others, synthetic organic resins. But you need a so-called thermo-set, like phenol-formaldehyde, which, once hardened, is resistant to further heating." At this moment, there is a knock on the door and a man in a white cloak enters. They talk in Urdu.

"I have to leave you for a minute, please excuse me."

N. is glad to have a moment to jot down the information of the raw materials. He would never remember it later.

Lakdawala is back and says that his foreman had some problems with one of the machines. But he was able to solve it quickly.

"Let us go and see my little factory," he invites N.

They start at the rooms where the raw materials are stored, all neatly labelled in drums.

"From where to you import these?" N. wants to know.

"The German company of Bayer," Lakdawala answers, "these are the very few times import licenses are granted to me, because the government issues import licenses mostly to Communist countries in eastern Europe and China."

N. finds the equipment spotlessly clean and well maintained and the machinery works almost silently with only a soft hum.

"As I said," N. remarks, "this is very remarkable. And what of other products besides household wares and army buttons?"

"I shall show you some samples in my office."

N. is thrilled to hear that. He feels to be near to what he has to find out.

Back in the office, Lakdawala opens a metal cupboard and takes out some round plastic object looking like a thickly disc, yellow-brown in colour, about 40 cm in diameter.

"What, for Heaven's sake, is that?"

Lakdawala takes off the lid and puts it back again.

"This is a plastic land mine, of course the outer case only. The army ingenieurs have to fill it, put in the detonators. This plastic mine does not corrode like metal casing would in time. And it is lighter to handle.

It will detonate by a weight of 20 kg. We supplied so far 2 millions."

"Phantastic," is all N. could say, "as a matter of fact that is exactly the right thing I need to put my washing gear safely away, because it is waterproof."

"Take it with you, then," Lakdawala offers and N. gladly accepts.

"But here is something else," Lakdawala takes out a small, round hollow plastic piece, red in colour with Chinese characters on it, about 4 cm in length and a diameter of about 2 cm. It has a sharp pointed spire.

"This is the point of a Chinese made missile which, fitted on the top of the weapon can be fired by individual soldiers. I have copied it, using extra hardened thermo-set. Here is a sample of our product.

"It must have taken some time and experiments to work out the copies."

"Yes," Lakdawala replies, "but I have good ingenicurs and chemists at my disposal. - And now let us have a quick tiffin lunch."

N. looks at his watch.

"That would be fine. It is already one o'clock, I have to pack, settle my bills, the plane leaves before midnight."

Lakdawala opens the little round boxes, five of them with hot food, one on top of the other, held by a contraption with a handle for carrying.

N. knows these tiffin boxes from India.

After lunch N. tells Lakdawala that he will concentrate on the tourism proposal and that they will be in contact through correspondence.

Lakdawala agrees and thanks N. for having come to see him.

N., all smiles, says he is sorry not to have brought him a present from Germany. Lakdawala at once asks N. what he would like for a farewell present.

It is now or never, N. thinks.

"If you can let me have one of those missile point as a souvenir, I should be very honoured."

"Of course," Lakdawala grabs one of the points from the cupboard and hands it to N.

Back at the hotel, N. packs his washing gear including a wet face towel into the land mine and for the valuable point he puts it into the round case which holds his shaving brush.

He is afraid that the customs officers at the airport may want to inspect his travelling bag when checking in.

He is relieved at midnight, sitting in the plane to Moscow and asks the stewardess for a stiff brandy.

Mission completed.

Back in Bonn "uncle" was most pleased with N's five pages long report and the "souvenirs" he brought back. A week later he received a bonus payment together with one litre of the finest Scotch whisky.

N. had spent the years from 1972 to 1974 with preparing his tourist consultancy. He had taken a small flat near Cologne and very near his German friend. It was a one-man office with telephone and a computer, the latter he learned to operate at the age of nearly fifty.

The advertisements he had distributed resulted in a number of enquiries and finally bookings from well-to-do clients.

ACROSS EUROPE, ASIA, AFRICA 1973

The first booking, in March 1973, was an incentive week-end to Cairo for 27 people spending the time with sightseeing and entertainment paid for by their company. It went well, they were satisfied with the Hilton Hotel, their excursion by coach (Pyramids of course) and the splendid entertainment at the Sahara Night Club.

End of the year he wrote a script for a documentary on Uganda for a German TV station. It was, after some passages had to be changed, shortened, altered, cut down to fifteen minutes, accepted and N. was asked to produce it as well. He at once contacted his old friend Rox who had done a number of documentaries with his camera and sound equipment. He agreed and the two went to East Africa. N., through his airline contacts received not only complimentary tickets but also free luggage allowance.

In Nairobi the whole material, cameras, sound equipment and a mountain of film rolls was held by customs. To release it for export to Uganda they would have to pay a deposit which they did not have. Thanks to the intervention of the German ambassador who issued a guarantee, they could proceed with a delay of two days in a hired car to Uganda, where Idi Amin was still in power.

It was a strange feeling for N. when they entered Uganda in Malaba frontier station and went on via Jinja to Kampala. N. had approached the Uganda embassy in Bonn before they left and had received a permit to film in Uganda in Kampala and the surrounding area up to Masaka. No other areas were permitted, but, as far as N's film is concerned, also not needed.

121

N. could not make out any changes in Kampala, and the road up to Masaka through parts of jungle was as beautiful as ever. It is the change of nature between Kenya and Uganda, N. explained to Rox.

"You see for yourself, Uganda is a country with lush green everywhere, Kenya has less of it, much more dry and sandy."

They made the film within ten days, N. went back to Nairobi with the exposed film rolls. Rox wanted to stay for another week to explore Uganda as much as he could with the camera.

Back in Germany, the TV people were astonished how two people can make a documentary in such a short time. They would need at least a team of eight or ten and twice the amount of days to do a documentary of fifteen minutes duration. The cutting was done in Wiesbaden at the studio, the film was shown about four weeks later. Eight weeks later the money arrived.

1973 N. took individual tourists several times to Kenya and Tanzania. March 1974, as reported, was taken up by his assignment to Pakistan.

The rest of that year N. accompanied clients several times to London and Corsica. 1975 N. was busy with small groups to Yugoslavia, Belgrade and the Adriatic Coast. 1976 N. guided only two tourists on a larger and adventurous tour to Bangkok, Hong Kong, Singapore and Kuching, the capital city of Malaysian Borneo. From there five hours by car first to Betong and another five hours, with an added translator, on a native dug-out canoe on the Scrang River, going upstream across raging currents and rapids, until they reached Tebat Longhouse amidst the jungle.

The clan chief of the Dayak tribe welcomed them on the longhouse, which was occupied by several families. On the bamboo walls underneath the thatched roofs hung a number of shrunken heads telling of the past when the Dayaks were headhunters. They slept on a very thin mattress on the bamboo floor, under it lived the pigs and chicken.

The question of conveniences came up.

"Toilet?" the translator asked and was shown down at the small clearing below: "Just go behind the bushes."

When it was N's turn, carefully stepping down the kerbed tree-trunk leaning against the longhouse and crouching behind a bush, he heard very loud snorting behind him. When he turned round, about five or six large pigs stood there, waiting to clean the floor. N. resolved not to eat pork anymore.

On the way back, dirty, unwashed, unshaven at the Kuching Hotel, they entered the reception hall filled with happy and dressed-up people attending a wedding on the premises. N. and his clients had four hour - long showers and baths in their rooms, before they looked respectable for the civilised world.

These were quite new experiences but N. decided to postpone his usual reflections about this wonderful and exciting venture. Now, there was no time to spare. The plane brought them back via Singapore to Germany.

1977 and 1978 there were more trips to Cairo where he and his clients stayed at the old historic Shepheard's Hotel. These times were dedicated to culture, to ancient Egypt and visits to the vast but rather dusty Egyptian Museum with its innumerable treasures. December 1978 up to January 1979 another of his tours took N. to Bangkok, Singapore and Sri Lanka. This time, apart of an elephant ride, the main activities concentrated on shopping.

Several other trips brought N. to the Emirates of Sharjah and quiet Korfakhan with its ten kilometre long white sand coast, tranquil and relaxing. But the interesting new experience for N. was a ten day tour to Burma. The military government allowed a stay of seven days only.

The bureaucracy started at arrival with a complicated and long lasting procedure: Each item of any value, such as wristwatches, a small alarm clock, a ring, a camera and others were painstakingly written on forms, the copy retained by customs, the original by the travellers, to be handed back at departure. Money was changed into local currency - all this took some hours.

The only thing not complicated were the people at the tourist office, which N. had contacted by mail prior to arrival. A minibus rushed the small group to the hotel in Rangoon, the old colonial building with the nostalgic interior: The Strand Hotel. Throughout their stay in Burma, the local guides, the drivers, the hotel staff everywhere were exceedingly friendly, polite and always smiling.

Going by old DC-planes to Taunggyi, to Heho, by car to the magnificent Inle Lake at dawn when the first sunrays kissed the rippling water and the fishmen on their canoes were silhouetted against the morning grey, walking up 375 steps to the great temple in Mandalay, looking at ancient stupas and temples in the vast area of Pagan and, another highlight, the enormous compound filled with numerous shrines around the majestic Shwedagon Pagoda.

Here, as in other temples, one could find whole families, with food rolled up in banana leaves, enjoying a quiet and happy picnic in front of smiling statues of Gautama Buddha. It struck N. that a place of worship was also used as a venue for family outings, including prayers, eating and even smoking hand-rolled cigars. To join together human life and religious devotion showed tolerance as well as respect.

It was an experience never to forget.

A very funny episode occurred on the last day of his stay in the Strand Hotel at dinner: The dining room was well filled, everybody enjoyed a meal and local beer, when, very solemnly, a big cat marched in proudly gripping an enormous rat, making its way straight into the kitchen.

Everybody observed this silently, when, all of a sudden, a laughter burst out from a table of Swedish guests into which all diners joined in.

A crowning event on N's last day in Burma.

Apart from the fact that "uncle" every Christmas sent a nicely wrapped bottle of whisky, N. only had a loose contact.

Now and then he was asked to purchase some items from a German producer which they would not or could not buy directly themselves for "diplomatic reasons." For example: a pocket spray for ladies to combat attackers to be purchased through mail order, or a particular section of the Chinese border from satellite photos obtained from the German Aerospace Industry, or a sample of bullet-proof vests to buy from the manufacturers, and so on. All perfectly legal and above board, and it was a nice side-income. In the course of the years there were several "uncles", Whenever, after two years in station, a new one was arriving, N. was introduced to them.

This went on until 1983, when N. developed a shoulder-arm-syndrome. It hit him so badly that he went from one doctor to another, trying acupuncture or a stretching therapy on a medieval looking contraption, but to no avail.

In that year N. read about the plight of the Tibetan people, suffering from the occupation of their land by China, the horrors of the cultural revolution, killings, torture, brutal suppression, the flight of the spiritual and secular head of government, the Dalai Lama, into exile in India. With him his government and some hundred thousand refugees, the formation of a Government-in-Exile in northern India.

He attended a convention, organised by Petra Kelly, the co-founder of the German Green Party, on the subject of Human Rights. The issue of Tibet was mentioned during the talks. N. met Petra Kelly afterwards and expressed his wish to help. They talked for hours, found similarities about the approach.

"The important thing," Petra told him, "is to make people aware that there are areas where human rights are trampled upon. Hardly anyone in Germany knows about the plight of Tibetans."

N. suggested to go to India, see the Dalai Lama, get his permission to start something like a Public Relation office. Petra Kelly agreed.

N. dropped his tourism business for the time being, contacted the office of the Dalai Lama, received after some week-long waiting an invitation, booked at once a flight to Delhi and travelled from there to the quaint little town of Dharamsala nesting below the snow-capped Dhauladhar mountain range.

LITTLE TIBET 1984

Well, it is India again. The plane arrived four hours late at six in the morning. No difficulties with customs on account of N's special visa from "uncle".

Outside, although early morning, brooding heat. A policeman hits a street urchin with his lathe. A snow-white cow roams between waiting buses and taxis. One of which drives N., after much haggling over the rate, to the York Hotel at Connaught Circus. It takes some time to find the hotel at K-Block. It is a small, well kept hotel with friendly staff.

At 8.30 he sits on the terrace outside his airconditioned room on the second floor and has, what is called a "continental breakfast": toast, jam, butter and a pot of most delicious tea. No tea bags.

Looking down at one of the main streets a chaotic traffic like in Bangkok, noisy and dusty like in Cairo, ruled by buses and motor-rickshaws. People look more serious, no signs of happy smiling like in Rangoon. They look harder. N. notices the difference from previous visits. On the other hand they seem to be consumer-conscious and impersonal. Dhotis are worn, if at all, at home only. The men wear trousers and shirts, in offices adorned with a tie. Most shops and offices are airconditioned. Only street cleaners and shoeshine boys wear dhotis. The so-called Nehru dress is not seen, the white congress caps are out as well. Women, at last, have not yet given up the sari.

There is an abundance of bureaucracy to obtain a train ticket for a sleeper. First you need a chit to get into the building. Once in you have to fill in a form complete with personal details, age, sex, nationality. Thirdly, on another counter, you get a note showing that you are entitled for a reservation. Lastly, at still another counter, you obtain the proper ticket for the Jammu-Tawi-Express, 1st class, sleeper from the main station at Old Delhi to Pathankot, high up in the north, leaving at eight in the evening, estimated time of arrival next day at about seven.

The news are encouraging. Terrorists had tried to lay fire on the station at Chandigarh, but were shot by railway guards. N's night express is to pass through Chandigarh.

Afternoon in Delhi, the first thunder. The city is covered in a mass of grey clouds. A storm howls, lightning and soon the clouds are opening and a Niagara-Fall-like water bursts on houses, people, vehicles and pavements. It lasts twenty minutes and all is over.

Fortunately prohibition has long gone. And the small hotel bar is well stocked.

At the entrance of one of the many cinemas a notice: No bags of any kind, no tiffin boxes are permitted inside. Police at the entrance look sharply. Bomb scares? Yesterday, according to newspaper reports, thirty-seven stations in Punjab province were set on fire. Obviously it is organised.

N. uses a taxi to old Delhi main station. Indescribable milling masses, small lanes, the main streets experience rush hour traffic every hour of the day. On the crowded platforms some attempts of demonstrations, railway guards and police are on the look-out.

N. has the company of an old Indian on the other lower bed. Before going to bed N. drinks from his thermos flask filled with tea at the hotel but laced with N's whisky. The old man opposite stretches out his hand.

"Have you some for me?"

"Of course," N. pours a little into a glass supplied by the Indian railways.

"Thank you," and the old man goes to sleep.

So does N. The soft rolling makes you sleepy. The world rolls, the circumstances vary every hour.

When he wakes, light streams through the unshuttered window, and the train moves slowly, clacking its wheels rhythmically, reluctantly uphill.

His left arm hurts and when he raises it a very severe headache, a migraine, makes itself felt, stretching from the neck to the front of his head. What a situation, to travel to the seat of the Tibetan government-in-exile and, perhaps, have an audience with the Dalai Lama. N. feels a bit desperate.

At all small stations the express train stops. Very far in the distance hilly country can be seen.

"Chai, Sahib?" the conductor appears and serves a glass of tea to the travellers. N. takes it with his right hand only. The pain from the left arm reduces if he does'nt use it. Finally the last station is reached.

"Pathankot, Sahib".

He hands a good tip to the conductor, takes his small case and the hand-all bag over the shoulder and steps onto the platform.

Soldiers everywhere.

A monk waives at him.

"Mr. N., Sir?"

"Yes,"

"I have been sent to bring you to Dharamsala."

But they wait for an hour before starting.

"I have to book the return ticket first," N. explains, because he had found out that the booking was done here without the complicated procedure of Delhi.

After that he goes to the washroom, has a wash and shave, then invites the monk to the station's restaurant to have a quick breakfast.

Off in a taxi.

Through Pathankot, the provincial town, he encounters much military presence.

"Is it always like that?" N. wants to know.

"Pathankot always has been a headquarter of the military in this area, even at the time of the British."

N. remembers the novel by Paul Scott "The Jewel in the Crown", this wonderful and exciting story of the times of the Raj, situated in this part of India. Scott has named the town in his novel Pankhot. But the description of his Pankhot actually matches Pathankot, this busy place, the streets lined by shops, the one cinema, the midan as well as the distant hills. The taxi drives through the settlement, past barracks, flagstaff house, the street sign "Club Road" - everything actually described in Scott's novel. "Amazing," N. thinks.

They go through an amazing landscape. Now, after the melting snow small rivulets had changed into gushing water-filled rivers, large rocks, lush green vegetation, in the far distance snow-capped mountain ranges appear, old stone bridges, on serpentines upwards- three hours lasts the ascend, they are now some 2400 meters above sea level. N. feels the height.

Finally they reach Dharamsala. The monk lets the taxi stop in a narrow lane.

"The Tibet hotel. Here you can stay and you will enjoy the best Tibetan food in town."

"I have to do something about my arm, there is a Tibetan Medical Institute, I believe. Could we go there?"

"Of course," the monk replies, "the taxi is still outside waiting for me. We can go there, my monastery is not far away."

The taxi takes them down some serpentines and again uphill.

"Dharamsala is stretching along several hills," he explains.

In a few minutes they reach the institute's compound. The taxi driver receives his fare and returns to Pathankot. On a verandah of the main building the monk explains that N. has to see a doctor urgently.

The nurse smiles at N. "You are lucky, the chief medical officer who treats His Holiness, is on duty. He is Dr. Wangyal. Please wait a moment."

The monk bids good bye to N.

"Over there you see the large compound with many buildings?" he says.

N. nods. "That is the seat of our government."

N. thanks the monk for his kindness, looking after him, and then follows the nurse into the consulting room.

Dr. Wangyal, smiling, invites N. to take a seat.

"Don't tell me your complaint," he says, "I shall find out."

And he takes three fingers of his hand to feel N's pulse on one hand, then does the same on the other. In full concentration, and it takes some time. He bids N. to take off his shirt and to bend forward. With one finger he probes down the spinal cord. At one part N. feels a twinge, the doctor takes a biro and marks the spot. He asks N. to lay down on the bed, puts a metal ring over the marked place, fills it with powder and lights it. N. feels a pleasant warmth on his back, lasting about twenty minutes, after which Dr. Wangyal lifts the ring, cleans the ashes and tells N. to sit up.

"Now take your arm right over your head."

N. does and is surprised to be able to do it without feeling any pain, without waves of aching across his head.

"How did you do it?"

"Quite simple," explains the doctor, "I gave you a Moksha treatment.

The burning of these powders over the source of your pain kills it. To remain so I shall subscribe you some pills for about 6 months. These Tibetan medicine you take three times a day. After that you will never have a severe headache or a migraine again."

N. thinks he has experienced a miracle and thanks Dr. Wangyal effusively.

As a fee is rejected, N. gives a generous donation at the counter outside where he receives the pills.

The pills have to be chewed, contain about natural ingredients, herbs, including micro-elements of sulphur, gold dust, iron and taste of bitter cardamom.

Overwhelmed and lighthearted N walks back - on foot - down and up again to the town center. Slowly, slowly because of the altitude, and without any pain.

A call has come during his absence and the receptionist gives him a note saying that a jeep will collect him at nine in the morning.

While having lunch, a rainstorm suddenly gushes powerfully from dark clouds over the town. The small streets and lanes become rivers. The strong wind gets hold of some loose corrugated iron roofs. One of them hits a car parked in front of the hotel and causes damage to the roof.

"Whose car is that?" N. asks.

"That does not matter," the waiter answers, "it belongs to an Indian."

The little dilapidated village, given to the Tibetans by the Indian government, has been restored by the refugees, they built stone houses, buildings, erected monasteries, the State archives, some are beautifully decorated, temples, with Tibetan style windows narrow on the top and wider at the bottom. The streets are filled with shops, run by Tibetans, there is a carpet factory, a primary school. Monks and lay people roam about busily. The few Indians look rather lost here. One very old shop still exists though, belonging to a Parsi, the post office and the banks are Indian of course, and the Indian government has even a liaison office with the Tibetan Government-in-exile.

The jeep arrives punctually to collect N. It makes its way through the narrow main street, turns right and follows a small recently tarmaced road to the office of the Dalai Lama.

Behind a high iron gate an imposing Indian Rajput guard in ceremonial dress with a stiffly starched part sticking out on top of his colourful turban. A Tibetan arrives, opens the gate and leads N. to a tiny security office. Inside, an Indian officer scrutinises N's passport. Then the Tibetan takes over and guides N. across a path into a room of the main building. A beautiful Tibetan thick carpet in beige and dark blue. Around the three walls wooden benches covered by carpets. Carved side tables with Tibetan designs.

In comes a Tibetan, introduces himself. Mr. Tsering, private secretary of His Holiness.

"We had some correspondence. Now we meet. But today I can give only five minutes."

And then - he arrives in his monk's robe: the Dalai Lama. He greets N. warmheartedly, laughs and sits down next to N. They speak about the refugee problem. N. has to deliver a donation cheque from the German Aid-for-Tibet office in Munich, Germany, to the Children's school, run by Mrs. Gyalpo, the Dalai Lama's sister.

Mr. Tsering takes notes and promises arrangements. N. hands over a letter from Petra Kelly.

"We need much more publicity", says the Dalai Lama and explains that Petra Kelly helps in the political sphere, but the public knows little about what has happened to Tibet. The five minutes are over quickly. Mr. Tsering fixes another meeting, this time an official interview for Monday at 13.30 hrs. A jeep will collect N.

On the way back to the hotel, N. has time to reflect. Even in this short time he felt the tremendous charisma coupled with joyful composure of the Dalai Lama, much more intensely as was his meeting with Krishnamurti. Krishnaji's approach was purely of the mind, the Dalai Lama's of kindness, compassion and humour. There will be a Tibetan wedding next day at the hotel, which normally takes about two full days for feasting, singing and dancing. N. decides to change into a quieter place and moves over to the small OM Hotel.

He gets the last simple room on a large terrace with the magnificent view of the green Kangra valley.

The room: One bed, one stool, some hooks for hanging clothes. Water, bath downstairs. Hot water one gets from buckets at the kitchen. All rooms bordering the terrace are like this. All are occupied by intelligent French, British and Swiss people. He phones the Dalai Lama's office about his change of address.

Dinner is served on the terrace: Tibetan vegetable soup with noodles and delicious Momos, steamed dumplings filled with meat and vegetables.

Very good discussions with the other guests, who are wonderfully different from the few hippies and youngsters, some with an extraordinary lack of general knowledge. (A German ask N. where is Srinagar?)

The Swiss couple are both medical doctors, have worked in Taiwan and have just come from working in refugee camps at the Thai-Camboja border region. Now in India they are going to work in Tibetan camps all over India. They agree that the friendliness of the Tibetans is a result of their naturalness, their simplicity which, in turn, is based on their religion.

A thunderstorm is brewing again. N. goes to bed early and appreciates his sleeping bag. It gets cooler and the pouring rain sings a lullaby. In the morning a jeep waits outside the Om Hotel to collect N. to the children's village. This is a huge compound with solid houses, 1400 children, teachers, workers, helpers. N. steps off the jeep slowly, the height is 2400 above sea level. Mrs. Gyalpo, the Dalai Lama's sister, looks after this large enterprise, while having tea with N.

"You should visit other, smaller schools," she suggests, "there are many others spread over India."

She points at the files which occupy two walls of her office. "Everything is noted down here."

"Are my two children in there too?" N. asks.

"Of course they are and you can see them in person soon."

N., through the German Aid for Tibetans, a humanitarian organisation put up by Mrs Waeger, who had received a Bundesverdienst-Kreuz, a medal to persons who have done charitable service for others, given by the Federal Republic of Germany, had adopted two children living now at the Tibetan Children's Village.

Mrs Gyalpo passes N. on to her secretary to show him around and also presents him to the two children, a girl, called Dechen, and a boy called Thubten. They do not let go of his hands when they were told that N. is their sponsor.

They are no orphans, their parents still live in occupied Tibet, but, together with adult others, went on adventurous ways, carefully avoiding Chinese border patrols, into India. The parents wanted them to have a good education including Tibetan and English but above all, to live under protection of His Holiness, the Dalai Lama.

N. gives a small lecture in a senior class, and, after a quick lunch, has to hurry down in the jeep to be in time for the audience.

There again a security check. At 13.30 he is led to the main building, this time with a ceremonial scarf which, according to protocol, he has to hand over to the Dalai Lama. His secretary explains that he has discussed his wishes to do lectures on the political aspect of the Tibet issue and to provide the media with news and background information.

After greeting the Dalai Lama and handing him the Kathak, he, with his deep and friendly voice, smiling at N., states: "I would not have any objection whatsoever if you open up an Information

Service with the object of distributing news, facts and figures on cultural, scientific and political aspects concerning Tibet to all media and the public in Germany."

He thanks N. in advance for his support which he would give to the Tibetan people and the Tibetan government - in - exile.

The preliminaries over, the audience concentrated on technical details, such as the communication through the Tibetan offices in Geneva, Paris and London, furthermore the background knowledge, historical and political, for which he will be instructed by the Minister of information. Mr. Tsering notes down what the Dalai Lama says. After thirty minutes he presents a very long silk scarf to N., when he sees N's camera lying on the side table he asks Tsering to make a photo.

Tsering takes the camera and tries, but the Dalai Lama, with a deep-throated laugh, shows him how to operate the camera and not to hold his hand in front of the lens. The second photo, this time sitting next to His Holiness, then takes N's arm and leads N. outside to the terrace.

Laughing and smiling, a third photo is made.

The audience is over. Outside, Mr. Tsering is waiting for N. and tells him that the Dalai Lama is sending a car which is to take him today to Kulu, a town seven hours away in Kulu Valley to see the small Tibetan School there. The car will take him next day to Chandighar where N. would get the night train to Delhi. Mrs. Gyalpo had arranged this. The car will collect him in 30 minutes. So N. has to be rushed to his hotel, pays the bill, packs.

N. feels this is the beginning of a new type of adventure.

On the dot a white car stands at the hotel. The driver, an elderly Kamba tribesman who has changed from horses to motor vehicles, explains that the car belongs to the car park of His Holiness unlike the jeeps which belong to the administration. The Kamba was one of the body guards who accompanied the Dalai Lama on his way into exile, dodging the Chinese troops across passes above five thousand meters through snow storms and winding paths to reach India. Unlike many Tibetans he is a very tall man, merry, always laughing and enjoying the cigarette lighter N. gave him.

With his cigarette dangling between his lips, he drives recklessly on endless serpentines with steep gorges on one and sheer rock on the other side of the small   road.   When a bus or a lorry approaches he stops, reverses to a spot where the road is a bit broader, lets the bigger vehicles pass and continues his hair-raising driving until, to the delight of N. they reach Kulu town at ten p.m.   From there to the school it will take another 20 km. They have a quick meal at one road-side Indian restaurant and continue.

At the school. late at night, they were waiting for them. N. gets a simple room with a bed, a stool and a table.   The sound of a nearby rivulet coming from the mountain and finding its way through the compound is a welcome lullaby. A dog lies at the door waggling its tail while half asleep.

Next morning, six o'clock, N. gets up, goes into the yard, uses the only water tap for washing and shaving. The children come out at 6.30 for puja and talks on their motherland, Tibet, in their language. Breakfast consisting of porridge, between 7 and 7.30. After cleaning their dishes, the students carry benches, desks and blackboards to the yard in front of their dormitories, school begins.

Dekyi Tashi, the school secretary and an old Lama, filled with compassion and friendliness show him around.   There are 266 children, between the ages from 4 to 13.   The buildings are 14 years old, run down and primitive. The very small children have a class room of their own, where Montessori trained teachers look after them. All others are taught in all subjects in English plus Tibetan and Hindi. About 45 children sleep in five crammed dormitories, looked after by ten teachers and ten house mothers. Besides the basic lessons there is work in the garden, cleaning and, together with the teachers, collecting fire wood.   This school really needs much financial help to build proper stone houses. N. noted down to include this subject into his talks in Germany, the photos he takes will illustrate the need for charitable help.

There are three cats, long-legged, and when N. purrs at them they speak back much to the astonishment of the Lama. N. gives his sleeping bag as a gift which is thankfully accepted.

At noon the Kamba driver starts the car and they are off to Chandigarh.

They should arrive there by eight in the evening to get the train to Delhi.

Downwards the serpentines, hairpin bends, the rock formations on the one side of the road are threatening to fall down, on the other side steep precipices - so they drive towards Punjab province. Right behind the provincial border the police controls start.

At one of the controls the police say that all is quiet in Chandigarh. Two days earlier a coach was stopped and the people inside were robbed by Sikh terrorists. They move on. At the fifth control they have to get out of the car. N's luggage is searched, it takes nearly one hour. Other cars are lining up. From the distance one can hear rifle shots. Some police men ran across fields with rifles and machine pistols. Then they are waved on. The sun sets at this time. Shortly before reaching Chandigarh another stop. This time for good. They say that they expect trouble in the town, therefore: curfew. No one can move. N. is definitely missing his train. They find a parking place near a petrol station. In an adjacent small eating place they have a meal of sorts and sleep in the car. It is quite cold in the night, no blankets, nothing but two jumpers, which N. and the driver can use. They get up at five in the morning, quick wash at the petrol station's tap. At six all cars are allowed to move on. No more controls. The Kamba drives N. to the bus terminal from where N. can get a coach to Delhi. There is only one train which leaves at midnight.

The bus leaves punctually at seven.

After 5 1/2 hours N. departs in Delhi, takes a taxi to his hotel, has a good breakfast, topping it up with a brandy, shower, shave, change of clothes. N. discovers that he is either too soft or getting too old or both to endure much strain.

One relaxing day in Delhi. Although there are still over six hours left before departure, N. decides to wait at the airport because it is climatised and Delhi simply too hot. He enters a conversation with another traveller who waits for his plane to Karachi. He has a cattle farm in Kenya and buys milk camels for breeding. He tells N. that the prices in Kenya have gone up by 300 per cent within seven years. They have tea together and he goes when his flight is called.

N. discovers a postbox which says that it will be emptied every hour.

N. sits there for hours and nobody came to collect the mail. Such is life in India. On the other hand the security check is very thorough. On the way to the gate a small beautiful mosque.

DIVERTISSEMENT

After his return from India, I saw N. in Germany. We talked for days on end on his recent experiences and especially about the Dalai Lama and his Tibetan Government-in-exile.

He seemed to be possessed of great inner joy. A feeling of goodness of life filled him.

"Meeting the Dalai Lama was one of those moments which come to people when they knew that what confronts them is the purpose, the task, the obligation which they, above everything else, have to do," he explained.

"I remember," I put in, "when we, long ago, talked of football you could not understand how twenty-two grown-up men made their money kicking a ball, and you felt pity with the ball to be kicked."

"Yes, because the ball is the underdog, and I always have a soft spot with the underdogs of this world," he replied, "in this case the underdog are the people of Tibet, kicked by their occupying masters."

He pointed to the heap of books, pamphlets, files, UN resolutions (which were not binding though), letters and statements of other countries regarding the plight of the Tibetan people, especially those of the USA.

"I have a lot of reading to do and start on my new job right now," he insisted, "contacting a number of people, not only in Germany, forming my own Information Service, and" he paused for a moment, "I need your help."

"Now look, you know that I am retired," I threw in.

"That is precisely why you have time to help. I have to see so many people, writing articles, preparing lectures, - I need you to look after my office when I am not around."

After lengthy discussions it boiled down to the fact, that I became a partner of his non-profit making enterprise, unpaid, of course. Petra Kelly, when he saw her, wholeheartedly supported him. She had succeeded to form an interparlamentarian Tibet Group together with MP's of nearly all parties, as had been done in France, Sweden and Britain.

There were about fifty-odd Tibetans living in Germany and they organised, with N. being present, a support group, called Tibet Initiative, duly registered by the German authorities.

"Things are getting faster than I would have thought," N. remarked.

"I have already invitations to give public talks in a number of places."

"It is a new phase in your life", I mentioned.

"If one is alert and agile, there always are several phases one goes through, that alone makes life so interesting." he acknowledged.

Although dealing with political issues, N. could not avoid to obtain a certain knowledge of Buddhist thought. He, per se, was not interested in any religion whatsoever which solely depend on institutions, on organisations, churches.

He was, he told me, interested in the origin, the sources of the teachings of prophets, wise men, mystics, although even these sources have been, in the course of history, censored, translated, changed, misinterpreted by even these institutions, councils, schisms to suit the "power policy" of the leaders of those institutions.

It was difficult to dig into the very origins, until he found out from a very learned Buddhist monk, Geshe Thubten Ngawang "Buddhism is the science of the mind."

This was an approach which suited N.: No prayers, no pujas, no visiting of temple services but contemplating on aspects of ethics like the Middle Way, Compassion, of analysing one's own thoughts, one's way of thinking, quoting Gautama Buddha: "Don't believe what I preach. Find it out for yourself."

These weeks went fast. I found a new N., serious, full of drive, with purpose, much work, inspired by Buddhist philosophy and the Dalai Lama's charisma. Still, he did not forget his humour. We laughed a lot, drank good wine and devoted our time to the tasks ahead.

On the 6th of July, 1984, at my home, the Tibet Information Service was officially inaugurated, in the presence of the press media and TV. Among the guests were the chairman of the Tibetan Association and the first secretary of the Indian Embassy.

As an energetic autodidact, N. learned about political thinking, analysed the hidden meaning of diplomatic language, polished his historical knowledge of Central Asia, of the mentality of its people and got hold through contacts of quite interesting facts, including even, what the Chinese authorities call "State Secrets".

These 14 years were filled with travels by train and planes to various places within Europe, culminating each year with visits to India.

These years were hectic, lectures had to be re-drafted, up-dated, because the political situation changed quite often. All this put an enormous stress on N.

The times spent in Dharamsala were mainly taken up with meetings of various officials and ministers of the Tibetan Administration, especially the Information Department with its head Lodi Gyari, who was well informed about the efforts of the Green Party.

Of course there were audiences with the Dalai Lama which N. could tape besides the taking of photographs. In 1985 it happened that the trip from Delhi was comfortable, but there was no way back.

The whole state of Punjab was closed for foreigners, large troop concentrations were posted along the border and even along the national border to Pakistan. The only way back to Delhi was to be by bus from Dharamsala to Delhi via Haryana State which was not affected by the ban to foreigners. The bus, with N. on board, left at ten in the night and reached, in a round about way, Delhi after fifteen hours and nine police controls. N. arrived at noon in the morning tired and shaken about by the bus.

Back In Dharamsala, 1986, there was a coming and going. The audience lasted only fifteen minutes, there were too many people waiting in the ante-room. There were discussions in depth with the Information Department, the Security officer and, in Delhi, with the Tibet Bureau there.

1987. Dharamsala again in May. The Information Ministry gave N. a wonderful dinner and presented him with a large and beautiful Thangka.

The audience with the Dalai Lama, scheduled to last twenty minutes, actually took forty-five minutes. N. could tape part of it, but for diplomatic and political reasons, the rest of the discussion was not meant for publication.

N. had the feeling that something was going on, something big. In Delhi lunch with Tashi Wangdi and a cocktail reception at the Tibet Bureau.

1988. No travel restriction in India any longer. Apart from another audience, there were meetings with the president of the Tibetan Youth Congress, the Tibetan Womens' Association, a visit to the Tibetan Institute of Performing Arts with a very impressive programme.

The Dalai Lama's policy of fostering Tibetan culture pays off. In most of the audiences in those years - there were eight altogether - they discussed political developments.

"People have the opinion that politics are bad," the Dalai Lama said, "but politics only have a bad image. And those who create this bad image are some of the politicians."

At other times they discussed aspects of Buddhism.

"I never try to convert people to become Buddhists. On the contrary I tell people of the West that they have a different upbringing, different religious traditions, thus should focus on that, perhaps trying to find similarities, especially in ethical teachings."

"Your Holiness," N. put in, "I recall that during one of your speeches in Germany, dozens of Western Buddhist followers were practically sitting on your feet. You came on the stage and told them "It also goes without religion.""

"Well," the Dalai Lama smiled, "you know that convertites usually take their new belief more fundamentalistic, more fanatic, more serious, but they forget that Buddhism in reality is peaceful, cheerful, happy and, above all, tolerant."

"Every Western person who has travelled in Asian Buddhist countries, can see the always smiling faces even if the people are poor," N. mentioned.

On another occasion they talked about the symbolism of the Indian and the Tibetan Government seals and flags. The Indian depict the Hindu/Tibetan Wheel of Life, guarded by two lions, the Tibetan show the Wheel of Life, guarded by two snowleopards. Both animals belong to the family of cats. It emerges that they both are cat lovers.

"I have a cat," the Dalai Lama said, "it so happened that my car was travelling up on this hill when I saw a small cat in a ditch, obviously sick and hungry. I stopped the car, got out and took the little creature in my arms, took it into my residence, called a vet. After a week it developed health and a shiny fur. She is living up there. Come, I will show you, but tip-toe like a thief, it is very shy."

He took N. by the arm and almost raced out of the audience room and, to the astounded body guards outside on the lawn, he led N. further up-hill to his residence.

And inside his residence there it emerged, a woolly small one sitting on the Dalai Lama's favourite arm chair. The Dalai Lama laughed like a happy child, photos were taken and they went down to the audience room. "This was great fun," he exclaimed. The body guards were relieved to see him back safe and sound.

In the afternoon N. walked down a hill to the small Anglican St. John's church and its old cemetery. The gravestones with inscriptions of British officers from the time of the Raj, the Victorian-style monument for Lord Elgin (the one with the Greek Elgin marbles). He was Viceroy and wanted to be buried here. An atmosphere like that of Scott's novels. 1989, N. was sitting quietly having lunch at the Baghsu Hotel, when a resolute lady walked in.

"You are my favourite spy!" she shouted laughingly and stopped at N´s table, who stood up, embarrassed and with question marks on his face.

"I am Vanya Kewley," she introduced herself, "I have just arrived from Tibet where I was filming secretly." She explained in detail that she had gone into the country as an ordinary tourist, left the other of the group and travelled, accompanied by two Tibetans by car via Kokonor Lake, Golmud, Naqchuka to Lhasa and back to Chengdu. Her film rolls she entrusted some other trustworthy tourists on their flight to London.

Well, she sure had a story to tell.

"But why do you burst in here and call me a spy in public?" N. asked.

"Because I read a book with your lecture in it, published in Berkeley, California, with all the juicy details on Chinese nuclear missiles in Tibet."

"You know that Lodi Gyari had asked me to go to Tibet. So I applied for a visa at the Chinese Embassy but it was refused. So I assume that I am persona non grata in the Peoples' Republic of China."

"See, what I mean?" Vanya said, "you have given away Chinese state secrets. Somehow you must have obtained documentary evidence about their missiles. So you are, in their eyes, a spy."

"The intelligence was given to me. I did not steal it."

"It boils down to the same thing. And even worse, it was made public.

Oh, what does one not do for the Tibetans," she explained, "in my case I filmed sensitive things, got the reels smuggled out of China and they will be shown next week on UK TV, channel 4."

"So we are birds of the same feather," N. remarked.

In the evening they had dinner together.

N's main activities, though, were in Europe.

Apart from numerous lectures at Tibet Support Groups in many towns and cities, in Germany, the Czech Republic, the Netherlands, where he mainly raised human rights, political issues and helping to get donations for construction of proper school buildings in Patlikul which, by the way, succeeded that this poor school got stone houses instead of those derelict wooden structures within a couple of years, he was giving lectures at universities, the Netherlands and - a highlight - a two-day seminar at Trinity College, Oxford.

And then there were numerous international conferences at The Hague, the European Parliament in Strassburg and Brussels, and in London. The latter was chaired by Lord David Ennals. There were rallies in Brussels and Geneva, Tibet Hearings in Copenhagen and Bonn, initiated by the Green Party with high-ranking delegates from the USA, from Great Britain, Sweden and others, where N. gave a detailed report on the developments of nuclear missile bases in Tibet with exact locations and their ranges, of airfields and stationed troops. He could not, of course, give away the sources - there were three - of his intelligence informations as that would mean not only to compromise them as well as himself.

At a demonstration with the attendance of some two hundred Tibetans from Switzerland, arriving in coaches, in front of the Chinese embassy in Bonn, it was quite an affair with German police trying forcefully to keep the angry Tibetans from climbing the embassy's fence. The windows of the main building were filled with eager Chinese staff taking photos and video shots. They most certainly got shots of N. who was in the centre of the melée trying to calm down the Tibetans.

Petra Kelly with collaborators of Chinese dissidents arranged a public hearing in communist East-Berlin which N. attended and met the dissidents who had come all the way from Paris.

Lodi Gyari and others from the Tibetan Administration from Dharamsala visited N's office near Cologne to discuss political and diplomatic issues and procedures.

The increased travels of the Dalai Lama to Europe and the USA, his public talks and meetings with officials, ministers and presidents made not only him but also the Tibet issue known world-wide. And most of the time he stopped in Germany where N. could help to assist his meetings, arranged some of the interviews and saw him more than on visits to India.

One day, having given a talk at the old Parliament building in Bonn and making his way to the exit, the Dalai Lama, seeing N. standing up at the aisle, stopped, greeted him shortly and whispered into N's ear: "I have a new cat."

He met the Dalai Lama, who was on his way to Oslo, in Berlin later, where he had to sign the Golden Book at the Lord Mayor's office. Protocol demands that next to the German the national flag of the visitor had to be on the table. When the entourage was about to enter, the Dalai Lama stopped short and refused to enter because, there on the table, was the flag of the P. R. of China. Quel éclat ! One of the Tibetan delegates mentioned that he had a small Tibetan flag in his hotel room. The Lord Mayor, very embarrassed, ordered a police car with blue light flashing to the hotel to collect the flag, which then was duly put on the table and the smiling Dalai Lama entered the office. Delay of the whole programme: nearly one hour which, in turn, delayed the luncheon reception. N. and Foreign Minister Tashi Wangdi, who sat together over the meal, felt in the best of moods.

After lengthy negotiations with the East-German government, the Dalai Lama was allowed to pass the check-point of the Berlin Wall into East Germany. This was a solemn moment when the exiled head of state, a burning candle in his hands, walked through with tears in his eyes.

But the culmination of all these years was, of course, the Nobel Peace Award in Oslo.

This boosted, more than anything else, the morale of all Tibetans within Tibet and exiled abroad together with their followers and friends world-wide.

The Chinese authorities were not amused and retaliated to brutally suppress any further demonstrations in Tibet. The news from Tibet were not encouraging at all. The demonstrations, mainly carried out by nuns and monks supported by lay people, led to severe clashes in Lhasa and other places to such an extent that the Chinese declared marshal law for nearly a year, only a few months before the happenings at Tianman square at Beijing.

It was the year of the "underdogs" but, in world opinion, not for the Chinese regime.

N. carried on, travelling from place to place. In Davos at the World Trade Conference (with Li Peng as main speaker) N. spoke at a separate conference hall on Tibet.

He took part at meetings of the European Parliament in Strasburg, where he met a fellow supporter of all underdogs in the world: Madame Mitterand. At a conference in Brussels he came to know Richard Gere as a serious, knowledgeable and able person fully committed to the Tibetan cause.

A new aspect of his activities came up when postgraduate students asked him for detailed information on different aspects on Tibet for their thesis. He helped out as much as he could and felt rewarded when they sent him their paper after having received their degrees.

His friend, in the meantime, had bought a flat on the island of Malta, first as a holiday flat, later as his permanent home. The Tibet Information Service came, as a branch office, with him to Malta, which N. visited occasionally too.

N. was by now 75 years old. The stress on him and his engagement of the last years made themselves felt and, finally, in January 1999, the reckoning came like a thunderbolt.

TIME FOR CONTEMPLATION 1999 - 2001

There was no pain, no symptoms of weakness, of exhaustion. But there was blood in his urine.

N. dashed to his practioner who diagnosed something serious after testing, but he wouldn't pinpoint unless X-rays were made by an urologist. Result: A fairly large tumour had nested in his bladder, which needed an operation at once.

N. had to enter a hospital, an experience quite new to him. He found the anaesthetic procedure most interesting. The exact timing, the awakening - he was always quickly awake without any kind of dizziness - was a process he found fascinating, reminded him of the Buddhist theory of re-incarnation being nothing but an activity of the continuating consciousness.

Four days later he was sent home to his friend's home where he was wonderfully looked after.

"There is something of a hospital bedroom that drains your self-confidence. One almost feels anonymous. And the food - better not to think about it." N. complained.

A week later he was due to the hospital again for a check. A second, smaller operation, was carried out, a second smaller tumour had been left on the wall of the bladder.

Another few days until he could rest at his friend's home. Regular weekly tests were done at the urologist's consulting rooms. He was told that the treatment would last two years with weekly, later monthly injections, but not at the hospital. They could be done at the practice rooms with the anaesticist present.

It was winter in Germany, anyway the time of short grey days, when leafless trees looked melancholic and people tend to be repressive.

Two years without stress. Time to contemplate, to think, to write, to follow news and political developments, to laugh, to get good food, drink good wines, to cuddle his friend's cat, to do some painting, to listen to music, to observe more: the purring of the cat, the twittering of early birds, the twilight waving soft shadows, the cracking of wood in the night, to listen to the birch tree at the front garden, swished by the wind telling you stories, to meditate, to have intelligent conversation in a cosy environment. Above all: to read and read and read and to learn.

Yes, to learn.

One never stops to learn if one is inquisitive enough. It is easy to think out questions - all children do that -, and the answers are contained within the questions, if one analyses the words, the meaning of words.

Ah - words!

"Words are seals of the mind. They are stations of unending phases of experience which have their origin in a far-away, inconceivable past, reaching into the present and are again forming new phases which are groping for an inconceivable far-away future."

N. recalled the words of the old Pygmy chief "The book is the magic of the white man". Books contain words.

"The hidden power of words was known to all wise men. They have known the origin of language.

The word became a mantra, a tool for thinking, a tool for creative further thoughts."

The very sound creates immediate reality. The sound of a mantra creates what IS, here and now.

OM, AMEN, AMîN, ALEPH -

Today, especially through the media, the spoken words are manifold, duplicated, multiplied thrown at us. Thus the value of words have reached their lowest point. This "new" language distorted the meaning of words. Some of the horrible distortions are, for instance, the word computer-speak (the verb speak being used as a noun,) what is the meaning of "hype", of "surfing the net, of "over-sexed" of "over-egged" of "to beef it up", or of "read" used as a noun?

But there are remnants of the knowledge of words still found in some Asian countries which have saved the mantric tradition still today, especially in one country: Tibet.

For the Tibetan it is not only the word, but every letter of the alphabet is a holy symbol, even if used in a profane way.

OM MANI PADME HUM.

But N's treatment phase was not only laziness. Besides much resting there were enough activities, concentrating on writing and answering letters, going with his friend's family twice a year to their new home in Malta. The office of the TIBET INFORMATION SERVICE there kept him busy. And, anyway, a new country made him meet new people, new helpers, new friends.

MALTA 1999 - 2003

The geographic position is by far not enough to get to know Malta. (There are five Malta's: Ohio, Montana, Idaho, Colorado, all in the USA) The one N. means is the tiny spot south of Sicily. It is very small indeed.

But "the Moon disappears when she has been big. The little stars go on shining although they are small."

And that applies to small Malta, the independent Republic with about 400,000 inhabitants: it is a star in the Mediterranean.

There are opinions which say, as a foreigner, one either loves Malta or one hates it. According to Aristoteles "a good judgement consists in loving and hating in the proper proportion." N. fell in love with the country, not necessarily with some attitudes some of its people show, especially those who speak of "their tradition".

Actually there is never such thing as black and white. There are always shades in between. Having to rely too heavily on tradition means to live in the past, which is often found in people living on a small island.

One of the so-called traditions is to shoot migrating birds. Some Maltese hunters shoot at anything that moves. They don't kill them for food, they just kill, even swans and flamingos, sometimes they give them to taxidermists.

The urge to shoot is, as every psychologist knows, a typical macho behaviour. Many men in Malta are machos even when they drive a car.

Though their homes are spotlessly clean, their streets are not (with exception of very small villages). Rubbish filled in bags are placed on the streets, instead of being put into skips. Those are stationed

154

in many places, are sometimes about 10 to 15 meters from the front door, but to reach them by walking is too much effort. They have no or very little feeling for animals, whether they are horses harnessed to hackneys standing in the hot summer sun without any shelter, or cats and dogs abandoned once they are grown and not wanted anymore, birds are often kept in cages too small for them. Rubbish bins on promenades or parks are rarely used.

Discipline is rather missing.

They are slightly anarchic, even in their political partisan activities.

Fortunately there are exceptions. There are quite a number of N's new Maltese friends who belong to the exceptions. Many look after animals and fight for the environment.

"How did these tendencies have developed?" is one of the questions N. asked himself. His answer: "Most probably due to historical experiences over generations." The history of Malta shows that it never was totally independent.

It was always occupied or, at least, influenced by people who happened to come to Malta. The semitic Phoenicians who had an impact on the grammar of Maltese language, the Romans, who, among others, exported the excellent honey from the island, but needed Malta as a military base against Catharge, the Arabs who dominated the land for about two hundred years and made their mark by introducing irrigation, bringing new plants and fruit trees into the island and, above all, greatly influenced the Maltese language (to about 85 %), the Normans came for a short time. Then Malta was occupied by the knights of Crusader fame who ruled the island from about 1530 to 1798. Malta was given to them by Charles Vth of Spain as a domicile having been defeated by Turks, Sarazens and Arabs in Palestine, and had, once they also lost Rhodes, nowhere to go. In 1798 Napoleon ruled for a few years.

He threw out the knights who then split: One strongly Catholic part left for Rome, the other via Poland to Russia where the Russian Orthodox Romanovs became their protectors and grand masters up to 1917.

(Today both branches of the knights have again their headquarters in Malta but do not play any political role.)

Malta, finally was occupied by the British until 1974 when it became an independent Republic.

The influences of all these "foreigners" have, of course, shaped the mentality, the attitudes, the behaviour of the local population, and only that development over centuries explains their way of thinking.

The greatest impact, though, is still that of the Roman Catholic Church.

Even today divorce is practically impossible. Many couples have separated and have to live "in sin" with another woman or man of their choice, although faithfully going to Church on Sundays. This creates some hypocrisy which is accepted by the people, not officially by the Church which seems to keep both eyes shut.

N. still loves Malta.

When asked "why?" he usually repeats his answer with a line from an old Arab saying which goes:

> "Do not complain because the rosebush has thorns.
> Be delighted that the thornbush carries roses."

N. finds some aspects of Maltese attitudes as being rather funny. And there are many stories to prove it:

One can observe people to cross themselves before entering a bus or their car and silently say a prayer to their God. Maybe even God would be praying watching the reckless drivers shifting gears. There is this wonderful story of a priest walking up to Heaven, but St. Peter did refuse entry. The priest astonishes when he sees behind St.Peter a man whom he recognised as a mere bus driver. "This bus driver," he shouts, "is in Heaven whereas I was faithfully saying Mass every day." St. Peter just smiled and told him: "When you said Mass, everyone went fast asleep.

Whenever the bus driver started the engine, every-one was praying."

Fortunately, there are a number of very good columnists working for Maltese newspapers who have a very good sense of satirical humour which N. likes so much.

156

The best ones are Daphne Caruana who does not mind to mince her words, and Raphael Vassallo who has a creative and comical way of writing, both are contributing for The Malta Independent.

"Why is it" writes Daphne, "that there are so many married women fat, so many unmarried women slender?

The unmarried women come home, look into the fridge and go to bed.

The married women come home, look who's in bed and go to the fridge."

Raphael writes about the fact that children up to at least thirty still live at home until they are married or forcibly evicted. One reason for this curious state of affairs is "that, unlike most other countries, Maltese students do not live on campus...it is standard practice for university students abroad to leave home and spend their college years living in dorms, digs, apartments or public parks. None of this applies to Maltese students (and not only students !)...dorms, digs, apartments are usually unavailable for rent...on account of the country's archaic rent laws and there are no public parks to speak of." No, the Maltese do not want "to forgo the many benefits of living with with one's parents...which includes your meals are cooked for you...the fridge is always full, clothes are always washed, ironed and neatly folded..floors are clean..."

N. laughingly thinks of that song "If you are good to mammy, mammy is good to you" from the musical Chicago.

Malta is a loveable funny country.

Although Maltese cuisine offers some excellent food especially a good variety of freshly caught fish and tasty bread and snacks like date-cakes, except perhaps for the preparation of vegetables which, a remnant of British occupation, and the British always have a peculiar relationship to food, and some even prefer to take in American-made junk food, Heaven's forbid. On the other hand, Maltese wines are superb.

Perhaps thanks to the arrival of Count Beaujolais in the 1800s and having introduced the making of good wines, who died here and has been honoured with a magnificent marble tombstone within the Valletta Cathedral. Only a very few tourist guide books mention this.

But really extraordinary is the baroque architecture in places like Valletta, the old city Mdina, in Victoriosa and some old palazzi spread over the country.

The fortifications of the capital city, also dating from the 17th century and the old watch towers dotted all along the coastline are most ingenious with their sturdy walls.

The yellow-brown houses of later times give the best impression of this country, because they fit into the scenery. Only the brand new structures, unfortunately, tall sky scrapers, steel, glass and concrete stand out as if they don't belong here. Which they don't. The bare rocks of Malta, the few spots of greenery, are a most impressive sight.

The neolithic temples at Hagar Qim and Mnajdra set against the blue sea and older than the pyramids, invite one to contemplate, to meditate, to reflect.

The yacht marinas bristle with armadas of masts, pompous yachts with names like Zarina, Ilderim, Bad Boy written in large letters on their polished sterns. Racing elegance with long pointed snouts. No, despite short-comings - also politically - Malta gave the idea, unusually for N., that he could settle here for the rest of his life. But was he already prepared for a decision? And how long would it take, this "rest"?

"I am too old, to play," he told his friend, "but I am still young enough to have dreams"

In Spring 2003 N. travelled to India again, "perhaps," N. said, "for the last time, just to say Good Bye to my many friends up in hilly, atmospheric Dharamsala." He left Delhi by express train first to Amritsar to say Good Bye to the fairytale-like Golden Temple mirrored in the artificial lake. The area between Amritsar and Pathankot full with troop concentration along the India-Pakistan border. From there by taxi via Pathankot, also there many troops on their way to Kashmir, to Dharamsala., where he had a talk with the Prime Minister of the Tibetan Government, Prof. Samdhong Rinpoche.

The Dalai Lama was, at that time, not there, he had arrived in Delhi coming from Australia. N. met him briefly at the airport, greeted N. warmly and remembered that they, apart from serious political discussions, had wonderful talks about the psychology of cats and their impact on human behaviour. They both laughed at this meeting and each wished the other, as it is Tibetan custom, a long life.

"Tashi delek".

EPILOGUE - MALTA 2004

"Well, we shall have a serious discussion about the book 'People and Places' which is, by the way, finished as far as your notes are concerned," I said.

N. and I were sitting comfortably at my flat in Malta. My wife was preparing our dinner in the kitchen, the afternoon sun shining into the living room.

"I suppose," N. said, "you have some things on your mind?"

"That's right," I agreed, "there are some points which have to be cleared."

"That means we have to talk about it," N. stated. "this has one disadvantage because 'one talks to hide one's thoughts' That was said by the philosopher Schleiermacher in 1835. He knew it, as he talked a lot."

I laughed and suggested an alternative: "We could make it like an interview. I question you and you may answer if you wish."

"That's good," N. answered, "let's start."

So I began.

"You have read the manuscript of your biography up to the year 2003. Do you think it will reach the reader?"

"Any biography, auto - or otherwise - is never written to deceive the reader. He can invent his own lies. But often it is written to deceive the author. Sometimes I think of my life as fiction. What we, in my case, have to consider is the psychological development in a person's being, his change of attitude during the course of time. I know that I have changed within these fifty years. But has the why come out properly?"

"Now you are asking a question," I replied, "I can see only that we all are the result of the past, family, upbringing, education, - all that what you call conditioning. Am I right?"

"Yes, you are. Many, if not most people, will remain conditioned. But one can, as I have learned through experience, to a great extent, be free from it."

"That is, where I don't quite agree," I remarked, "you left your country to see the world in a state of naivety, you just went. Let us call this phase one. But inside yourself you had this conditioned mind it was then, let us say, disturbed by the philosopher Krishnamurti. Is that not one new form of conditioning propped up upon the old one?"

"In a way, it is," N. agreed, "experience means forming the behaviour pattern in later years. Krishnamurti made at least the old conditioning crumble, because he made his listeners know that they are conditioned, living in the past. The adherence to this past has been shaken, but, I admit, not totally destroyed."

"Krishnamurti has, therefore, made you see, given you a new outlook on things, made you more aware? Can we call this change phase two?"

"Yes," N. answered, "awareness is the result of his teachings. Awareness of that what IS. Even looking around, being actually aware what you see, touch, smell, hear. Your outlook on your surroundings changes."

"But still, were you not working and living as before?"

"Naturally, the physical needs cannot be laid aside. You have to get food, shelter, clothes. These are necessities. I told you once before, that Krtishnamurti approaches from an intellectual point of view. He simply sharpens your mind. That would be the first step of any change. And that, really, has started phase two in my life."

I filled our glasses again. "And then, in Pakistan, you seem to have been thrown back. You participated in espionage in order to receive a lot of money without thinking of philosophy. Was it experience of excitement for excitement's sake?"

"I would say: for experience's sake. That it was connected with excitement made it more interesting. I wanted to find out what will happen to my way of thinking, if I deal with something new,

162

I had never even considered before. But I still had the power of observation, of being aware.

Yes, and it was fun. I did not hurt anyone, except the budget of certain governments, but that was surely a micro-tiny bit of their overall expenditure. Often they have to pay enormous sums for intelligence which is faked. The intelligence regarding weapons of mass destruction were based on false information. My information proved to be absolutely correct."

"Let us number this type of experience phase three, after all, it lasted, at least what your dealings with all the "uncles" were concerned, in a much smaller and legal scale, up to about 1998. And then came your tourism activities, seeing many new countries and meeting new people, that would be stage four."

"Although," N. put in, "it was overlapped by phase number five which had by far the greatest impact on my attitude and way of thinking."

"I agree," I said, "with phases one to four slowly fading out, the new phase started due to your experience of a people in dire need for help.

Was it your discovery of Buddhist philosophy or of the impact of the Dalai Lama?"

"These two went together. When I talked to His Holiness, it was not on Buddhism, it was on the plight of his people who had been practically abandoned by the world consciousness, mainly due to the fact that the media, nourished by bloodshed, forgot all about Tibet. If there is no blood shown on TV, it is not news. And the big powers did not do anything. There is no oil in Tibet. Tibet is not Iraq.

The Dalai Lama, for me, is the impersonation of compassion. He preaches peace and he lives it. He had to convince, especially the young Tibetans, never to resort to violence. That, after all, brought him the Nobel Peace Prize.

"They spend billions of dollars to wage a war," he told me, "but when I ask for peace, they laugh at me."

Politically he appears, sometimes, naive, like a child. Many people put their childhood, their naivety into a locked suitcase. Very few reopen that suitcase and bring it out again.

The belly-laughter of his personality, on occasions, when you don't expect it, is some sort of unlocking. That, combined with his rather overwhelming charisma and his clear thinking make him, for me, a person who has fulfiled man's possibility to live in clarity in this confused world."

At this stage we smelled mouth-watering whiffs of garlic, ginger and curry. And my wife calling: "Dinner in five minutes."

We got up and proceeded to the dining room.

After a delicious spicy Indian soup (carrots, ginger, freshly pressed orange and lemon juice, spices and one potato), my wife served a lamb curry, with raita, ice-cold yogurt, mango chutney and rice.

After dinner we sat on the balcony to finish our wine. The question and answer session went on.

"Normally," I started, "a biography should begin right at the beginning, birth where and when -"

" - and why?" N. interrupted mischievously.

" - and parents, home, upbringing, schooling and so on," I continued with a smile.

"There is not much I can say. At my birth I was present, naturally, but I do not remember anything."

"What then is the oldest memory you have?" I enquired.

""I was sitting in a pram, holding out one arm and my hand touched or stroke our Alsatian dog trotting along on the side of my pram.. May be that, from this early experience, I developed a liking for furry animals."

"I am sure of it," I interrupted.

"From my father I recall from one of his stories, that he was an expert of milking grazing cows. No, he was, at that time, not yet my father and he never was a farmer. This happened during the first World War in 1916, and the cows grazed in No-Man's-Land between the frontlines in France. He told me this story many times, and I found it very funny.

When there was a lull in the shooting between the trenches, my father would crawl out of his to reach a cow and milk it. One day he had the splendid idea to catch one cow and push it to his trench. But the cow was not in favour of this and started to low, to moo.

The other cows fell in and the French of the other side became suspicious and started to shoot.

My father never got a medal for his heroic deed to supply fresh milk for him and his comrades.

Many years later, when I grew up, as a teenager he gave me a number of advices, such as 'Never to take up a loan. Always to save up and pay cash.'

and 'when you go out into the world always look at mountains from below, Churches from outside and pubs from inside.' And also: 'Don't marry before you have your first stroke, and then a nurse!'

Well, I followed the first, for the third I have not quite reached that stage."

"I can imagine," I said, "that your sense of humour must have been derived from those stories?"

"It may well be," N. replied.

"There is one period we haven't covered yet: What did you do during the Second World War?"

"I survived."

I was caught end of 1944. I had managed not being drafted up to then quite successfully by devious means which I don't want to reveal. But then I was pressed into uniform and, first thing, I had to learn how to salute, and that while a furious war was on. Walking about in uniform I had not the faintest notion whom and when to salute. You were punished if you missed anyone above your plain rank. To be on the safe side I saluted anyone wearing a uniform, even a postman.

Finally I was posted to Holland.

My whole military time was a period when I went into intellectual hibernation for the duration.

I have learned from this war-time experience to decline worrying about things over which I have no control."

The stars above the Maltese sky had come out in force, a mellow breeze shook the flame of the candle. The last glass of wine was drowned.

The next day, after breakfast, we sat in my booklined study. Our discussion continued.

165

"Now we have to talk about women and love."

"I thought that this will have to come," N. sighed, "at least to satisfy the sex-hungry public, - I am free emotionally, I did not think of marriage. I wanted to travel, see places, meeting people. I was the wrong man for the majority of women I met. My sense of independence was too great.

Now, at this age, I have forgotten to think of sex for a long time."

"Is that perhaps a sign of maturity and dignity of old age and decay?" I asked him.

"May be it is all of them," N. replied." The very routine of courtship for me is a waste of energy. Anyway, as someone once said, 'it is two percent inspiration and ninety-eight percent perspiration,'" he laughed.

"- and " he continued, "love? The ancient Greeks thought that love is a child of chaos.

To love has to do with passion. Do you know what it means to be passionately in love? Passion derives from Latin and means suffering.

The Latin root is passus and pati, meaning to endure. Being in love indicates to suffer but also to endure the suffering.

And then this childish wish to want to belong to someone. Nobody can claim to possess someone.

Cats are much wiser: They never think even that you possess them. They, on the contrary, possess you. Your lovely cat here at your home owns you. This home is not yours. You are, in the cat's mind, a tenant.

They endure you only because you are providing nourishment.

These are my independent views whether you, my friend, or the reader like them or not.

As far - and these are my final words on this subject - as I am concerned - I like to embrace a good book, and I love to read a woman."

"Last request," I asked, "can you, briefly, tell me which of the thirty countries you visited, some of them several times, had made the greatest impression on you?"

"There are, I think, ten - not the entire countries, but some individual sights - I could mention.

166

In Egypt, the Egyptian Museum and the Pyramids at sunset. In India, Ravi Shankar's concert under the huge Banyam-tree in Adyar, in Dharamsala in the North the smell of Himalaya pines and the snow-capped mountains of the Dauladar Range.

In Kenya the Naivasha Lake in the morning with millions of flamingos forming a pink cloud over the water.

In Iran the midan at Isfahan with its beautiful architecture.

In Iraq the outstanding Iraqi Museum in Baghdad.

In Britain the Cathedral in Durham with its massive and powerful columns.

In Tanzania Mount Kilimanjaro at sunset with pink reflection on the snow peak.

In Burma the sound of little bells on the temple roofs in Taungyi at sunset, the Inle Lake at sunrise with the silver sparkles on the water, and the Shwedagon Pagoda in Rangoon.

In Malta the neolithic temples Hagar Qim and Mnajdra and the "silent' city Mdina.

"And of all the many people you have met, which would you name to have had the most impact on you?"

"Well, that is quite a question," N. replied thoughtfully, "In India Krishnamurti, of course, as I learned clarity and awareness through him."

In Germany Petra Kelly who, as a politician, worked hard for the Tibetan cause, nearly to exhaustion.

In Australia Jan Locher, who proved to be a reliable friend and brilliant conversationist, besides being an excellent chess player.

In Belgium, during an EU-meeting, Richard Gere for his serious and determined commitment for Tibet.

In India, Tenzin Gyatso, the 14th Dalai Lama of Tibet.

But there are countless more, from helpful taxi-drivers to interested tourists and politicians.

Let me just add some thought: We learned about the seven wonders of the world. In my opinion, these "wonders" are basically materialistic architecture. In my understanding, the Seven Wonders of the human World should be: (1) To see, (2) to hear, (3) to touch, (4) to taste (5) to feel, (6) to think, (7) to laugh."

"Now," I concluded, "we have discussed People and Places and the different phases you underwent. Can we expect a new phase in future?"

"I do not look at the future," N. answered, "I prefer to look at the present. One day is the time from sunrise to sunset. One month is measured by the moon and the planets. Time, therefore, is measured by the difference between two specific movements. There, actually, is no time per se."

I think I shall certainly meet a few more people and places. The wish-list of my dreams is not quite crossed off. -

"At this point I like to tell you a little story from ancient China: 'I dreamt I was a butterfly. When I awoke, I did not know have I dreamt to be a butterly, or am I a butterfly who now dreams he is a human?"

This story has, for many times, be a leitmotif for my way of life. To answer your question: I shall be back, soon or in my next life, because I live, I lived and re-live, either as a human or a butterfly, who knows?

So, my friend and now I say to you and the readers: Good Bye, Adieu, Auf Wiedersehen, naga naghrak, totziens, kwaheri, allah-is maladiq, do swidanya, ciao, sayonara, tashi delek."

Two days after this discussion, N. left Malta with a small suitcase. But I am sure, he will be back.

LIST OF WORDS

Bwana (Swaheli) — Mister, Sir (page 118)

Chaikhana (Parsi) — small tea house (page 88)

Chaukidar (Urdu/Hindi) — Night watchman (page 44)

Choli (Hindi) — tight bolero-like jacket (page 37)

Dhobi (Urdu/Hindi) — Washerman (page 35)

Essalaam aleikum (Arab) — Peace be with you (page 10)

G. R. U. (Russian) — Directorate for Military Intelligence (page 43)

Kathak (Tibetan) — Ceremonial silk scarf (page 151)

K. G. B. (Russian) — Espionage and counter espionage (page 33)

Midan (Arabic) — Town square (page 11)

Om mani padme hum (Tib./Sanskrit) literally: "To the secret of the Lotus", symbolizing human evolution, starting from the root in the mud of the sea-bed, growing through the water, reaching the air and budding, evolving as full flower by the touch of the sun = enlightenment (page 169)

Puja (Hindi) — Prayer (page 152)

Raita (Hindi) — Salad with cucumber, onions, yogurt (page 180)

Raj (Hindi) — King, ref. to British rule in India (page 30)

Shamba (Swahili) — Small plot of land (page 86)

Tabla (Hindi/Urdu) — small drum (page 38)

Tashi delek (Tibetan) — Good luck-wish (page 175)

Tiffin (Hindi/Urdu) — Breakfast, lunch (page 39)

Tika (Hindi) — A sign painted between the eyebrows (page 37)

Travelling afar -
befriending wise men -
respecting beautiful women -
entertained by King's Courts -
enlightened by good books -
that means: to live.

Sri Kabir,
India, 13th Century.

CREDO - A Book for the very few - By Norman Lowell

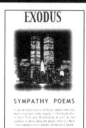

EXODUS - *Poems dedicated to the 11th September victims -* by Various authors

A PAWN FOR THE QUEEN - By Ken Lake *(Novel/Thriller)*

VILLA BLYE - When we were young - by Bro. Douglas Shields *(Masonic)*

WHICH COURSE? - *(Directory)*

MALTA'S PUBLISHING & MEDIA HANDBOOK - *(Directory)*

IL-QANPIENA TA' NOFS IL - LEJL - by David James. Translated by Alfred Palma

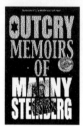

OUTRCRY - by Manny Steinberg *(Autobiography) A holoucast survivor*